ALEX LA GUMA was born in 1925, son of one of the leading figures in the non-white liberation movement. As a young man he joined the Communist Party, and was a member of its Cape Town district committee until 1950, when it was banned. In 1956 he helped to organize the South African representatives who drew up the Freedom Charter, and consequently was among the 156 accused at the Treason Trials of the same year. In 1960 he began writing for *New Age*, a progresssive newspaper, and in 1962 was put under house arrest. Before his five year sentence could elapse, a No Trial Act was passed and he and his wife were put into solitary confinement. On their release from prison, they returned to house arrest, eventually fleeing to Britain in 1967. They moved to Cuba, where La Guma was the ANC representative. He died in 1985.

Alex La Guma's first work was *A Walk in the Night*, (1962), a collection of short stories. It was followed by *And a Threefold Cord*, *The Stone Country*, *The Fog in the Seasons' End*, and *The Time of the Butcherbird*.

ALEX LA GUMA

A WALK IN THE NIGHT

AND OTHER STORIES

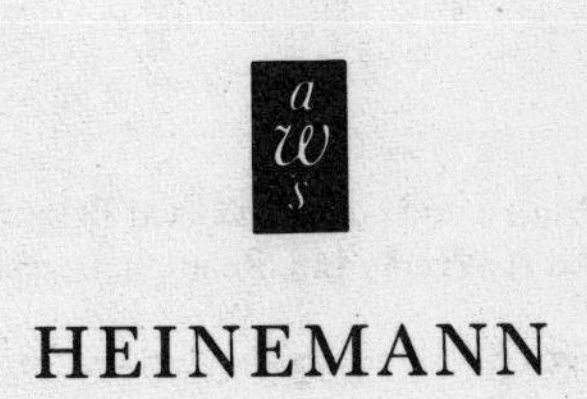

HEINEMANN

Heinemann Educational Publishers
A division of Heinemann Publishers (Oxford) Ltd
Halley Court, Jordan Hill, Oxford OX2 8EJ

Heinemann: A division of Reed Publishing (USA) Ltd
361 Hanover Street, Portsmouth, NH 03801-3912, USA

Heinemann Educational Books (Nigeria) Ltd
PMB 5205, Ibadan
Heinemann Educational Boleswa
PO Box 10103, Village Post Office, Gaborone, Botswana

FLORENCE PRAGUE PARIS MADRID
ATHENS MELBOURNE JOHANNESBURG
AUCKLAND SINGAPORE TOKYO
CHICAGO SAO PAULO

A Walk in the Night first published by Mbari Publications 1962
Tattoo Marks and Nails and Blankets first published in *Black Orpheus*, 1964
At the Portagee's first published in *Black Orpheus*, 1963

The Gladiators, A Matter of Taste and *The Lemon Orchard* first published 1967

This collection first published 1967
First published in African Writer's Series as AWS 35, in 1968

British Library Cataloguing in Publication Data

La Guma, Alex
A walk in the night and other stories.
(African writers series; 35)
I. Title II. Series
823[F] PR9369.3.L3

ISBN 0-435-90754-9

Printed and bound in Great Britain by
Cox & Wyman Ltd, Reading, Berkshire

95 96 97 98 10 9 8 7 6

CONTENTS

A Walk in the Night *1*

Tattoo Marks and Nails *97*

At the Portagee's *108*

The Gladiators *114*

Blankets *121*

A Matter of Taste *125*

The Lemon Orchard *131*

FOR
Tyres, Gogs, AND *Italiaan*

I am thy father's spirit;
Doom'd for a certain term to walk the night,
And for the day confined to fast in fires,
Till the foul crimes done in my days of nature
Are burnt and purged away.

WILLIAM SHAKESPEARE: *Hamlet, Act I, Scene V*

A Walk in the Night

ONE

The young man dropped from the trackless tram just before it stopped at Castle Bridge. He dropped off, ignoring the stream of late-afternoon traffic rolling in from the suburbs, bobbed and ducked the cars and buses, the big, rumbling delivery trucks, deaf to the shouts and curses of the drivers, and reached the pavement.

Standing there, near the green railings around the public convenience, he lighted a cigarette, jostled by the lines of workers going home, the first trickle of a stream that would soon be flowing towards Hanover Street. He looked right through them, refusing to see them, nursing a little growth of anger the way one caresses the beginnings of a toothache with the tip of the tongue.

Around him the buzz and hum of voices and the growl of traffic blended into one solid mutter of sound which he only half-heard, his thoughts concentrated upon the pustule of rage and humiliation that was continuing to ripen deep down within him.

The young man wore jeans that had been washed several times

and which were now left with a pale-blue colour flecked with old grease stains and the newer, darker ones of that day's work in the sheet-metal factory, and going white along the hard seams. The jeans had brass buttons, and the legs were too long, so that they had to be turned up six inches at the bottom. He also wore an old khaki shirt and over it a rubbed and scuffed and worn leather coat with slanting pockets and woollen wrists. His shoes were of the moccasin type, with leather thongs stitching the saddle to the rest of the uppers. They had been a bright tan once, but now they were worn a dark brown, beginning to crack in the grooves across the insteps. The thongs had broken in two places on one shoe and in one place on the other.

He was a well-built young man of medium height, and he had dark curly hair, slightly brittle but not quite kinky, and a complexion the colour of worn leather. If you looked closely you could see the dark shadow caused by premature shaving along his cheeks and around the chin and upper lip. His eyes were very dark brown, the whites not quite clear, and he had a slightly protuberant upper lip. His hands were muscular, with ridges of vein, the nails broad and thick like little shells, and rimmed with black from handling machine oil and grease. The backs of his hands, like his face, were brown, but the palms were pink with tiny ridges of yellow-white callouses. Now his dark brown eyes had hardened a little with sullenness.

He half-finished the cigarette, and threw the butt into the garden behind the fence around the public convenience. The garden of the convenience was laid out in small terraces and rockeries, carefully cultivated by the City Council, with many different kinds of rock plants, flowers, cacti and ornamental trees. This the young man did not see, either, as he stepped off the pavement, dodging the traffic again and crossing the intersection to the Portuguese restaurant opposite.

In front of the restaurant the usual loungers hung around under the overhanging verandah, idling, talking, smoking, waiting. The window was full of painted and printed posters advertising dances, concerts, boxing-matches, meetings, and some of the loungers stood looking at them, commenting on the ability of the fighters or the popularity of the dance bands. The young man, his name was Michael Adonis, pushed past them and went into the cafe.

It was warm inside, with the smell of frying oil and fat and tobacco smoke. People sat in the booths or along a wooden table down the centre of the place, eating or engaged in conversation. Ancient strips of flypaper hung from the ceiling dotted with their victims and the floor was stained with spilled coffee, grease and crushed cigarette butts; the walls marked with the countless rubbing of soiled shoulders and grimy hands. There was a general atmosphere of shabbiness about the cafe, but not unmixed with a sort of homeliness for the unending flow of derelicts, bums, domestic workers off duty, in-town-from-the-country folk who had no place to eat except there, and working people who stopped by on their way home. There were taxi-drivers too, and the rest of the mould that accumulated on the fringes of the underworld beyond Castle Bridge: loiterers, prostitutes, *fah-fee* numbers runners, petty gangsters, drab and frayed-looking thugs.

Michael Adonis looked around the cafe and saw Willieboy sitting at the long table that ran down the middle of the room. Willieboy was young and dark and wore his kinky hair brushed into a point above his forehead. He wore a sportscoat over a yellow T-shirt and a crucifix around his neck, more as a flamboyant decoration than as an act of religious devotion. He had yellowish eyeballs and big white teeth and an air of nonchalance, like the outward visible sign of his distorted pride in the terms he had served in a reformatory and once in prison for assault.

He grinned, showing his big teeth as Michael Adonis strolled up, and said, 'Hoit, pally,' in greeting. He had finished a meal of steak and chips and was lighting a cigarette.

'Howzit,' Michael Adonis said surlily, sitting down opposite him. They were not very close friends, but had been thrown together in the whirlpool world of poverty, petty crime and violence of which that cafe was an outpost.

'Nice, boy, nice. You know me, mos. Always take it easy. How goes it with you?'

'Strolling again. Got pushed out of my job at the facktry.'

'How come then?'

'Answered back to a effing white rooker. Foreman.'

'Those whites. What happened?'

'That white bastard was lucky I didn't pull him up good. He had been asking for it a long time. Every time a man goes to the piss-house he starts moaning. Jesus Christ, the way he went on you'd think a man had to wet his pants rather than take a minute off. Well, he picked on me for going for a leak and I told him to go to hell.'

'Ja,' Willieboy said. 'Working for whites. Happens all the time, man. Me, I never work for no white john. Not even brown one. To hell with work. Work, work, work, where does it get you? Not me, pally.'

The Swahili waiter came over, dark and shiny with perspiration, his white apron grimy and spotted with egg-yolk. Michael Adonis said: 'Steak and chips, and bring the tomato sauce, too.' To Willieboy he said: 'Well, a juba's got to live. Called me a cheeky black bastard. Me, I'm not black. Anyway I said he was a no-good pore-white and he calls the manager and they gave me my pay and tell me to muck of out of it. White sonofabitch. I'll get him.'

'No, man, me I don't work. Never worked a bogger yet. Whether you work or don't, you live anyway, somehow. I haven't starved to death, have I? Work. Eff work.'

'I'll get him,' Michael Adonis said. His food came, handed to him on a chipped plate with big slices of bread on the side. He began to eat, chewing sullenly. Willieboy got up and strolled over to the juke-box, slipped a sixpenny piece into the slot. Michael Adonis ate silently, his anger mixing with a resentment for a fellow who was able to take life so easy.

Music boomed out of the speaker, drowning the buzz of voices in the cafe, and Willieboy stood by the machine, watching the disc spinning behind the lighted glass.

When mah baby lef' me,
She gimme a mule to rahd . . .
When mah baby lef' me,
She gimme a mule to rahd . . .

Michael Adonis went on eating, thinking over and over again, That sonavabitch, that bloody white sonavabitch, I'll get him. Anger seemed to make him ravenous and he bolted his food. While he was drinking his coffee from the thick, cracked cup three men came into the cafe, looked around the place, and then came over to him.

One of the men wore a striped, navy-blue suit and a high-crowned brown hat. He had a brown, bony face with knobby cheekbones, hollow cheeks and a bony, ridged jawline, all giving him a scrofulous look. The other two with him were youths and they wore new, lightweight tropical suits with pegged trousers and gaudy neckties. They had young, yellowish, depraved faces and thick hair shiny with brilliantine. One of them had a ring with a skull-and-crossbones on one finger. The eyes in the skull were cheap red stones, and he toyed with the ring all the time as if he wished to draw attention to it.

They pulled out chairs and sat down, and the man in the striped suit said: 'Het, Mikey.'

'Hullo.'

'They fired me.'

'Hell, just near the big days, too.' The man spoke as if there was something wrong with his throat; in a high, cracked voice, like the twang of a flat guitar string.

The boy with the ring said, 'We're looking for Sockies. You seen him?'

The man in the striped suit, who was called Foxy, said, 'We got a job on tonight. We want him for look-out man.'

'You don't have to tell him,' the boy with the ring said, looking at Foxy. He had a thin, olive-skinned face with down on his upper lip, and the whites of his eyes were unnaturally yellow.

'He's okay,' Foxy told him. 'Mikey's a pal of ours. Don't I say, Mikey?'

'I don't give over what you boys do,' Michael Adonis replied. He took a packet of cigarettes from the pocket of his leather coat and offered it around. They each took one.

When the cigarettes were lighted the one who had not spoken yet, said: 'Why don't we ask him to come in? We can do without Sockies if you say he's okay.' He had an old knife scar across his right cheekbone and looked very young and brutal.

Michael Adonis said nothing.

'Mikey's a good boy,' Foxy said, grinning with the cigarette in his mouth. 'He ain't like you blerry gangsters.'

'Well,' said the scarfaced boy. 'If you see Sockies, tell him we looking for him.'

'Where'll he get you?' Michael Adonis asked.

'He knows where to find us,' Foxy said.

'Come on then, man,' the boy with the scarface said. 'Let's stroll.'

'Okay, Mikey,' Foxy said as they got up.

'Okay.'

'Okay, pally,' the scarfaced boy said.

They went out of the cafe and Michael Adonis watched them go. He told himself they were a hardcase lot. The anger over having got the sack from his job had left him then, and he was feeling a little better. He picked up the bill from the table and went over to the counter to pay it.

Outside the first workers were streaming past towards Hanover, on their way to their homes in the quarter known as District Six. The trackless trams were full, rocking their way up the rise at Castle Bridge, the overflow hanging onto the grips of the platform. Michael Adonis watched the crowds streaming by, smoking idly, his mind wandering towards the stockinged legs of the girls, the chatter and hum of traffic brushing casually across his hearing. Up ahead a neon sign had already come on, pale against the late sunlight, flicking on and off, on and off, on and off.

He left the entrance of the cafe and fell into the stream, walking up towards the District, past the shopfronts with the adverts of shoes, underwear, Coca-Cola, cigarettes.

Inside the cafe the juke-box had stopped playing and Willieboy turned away from it, looking for Michael Adonis, and found that he had left.

TWO

Up ahead the music shops were still going full blast, the blare of records all mixed up so you could not tell one tune from another. Shopkeepers, Jewish, Indian, and Greek, stood in the doorways along the arcade of stores on each side of the street, waiting to welcome last-minute customers; and the vegetable and fruit barrows were still out too, the hawkers in white coats yelling their wares and flapping their brownpaper packets, bringing prices down now that the day was ending. Around the bus-stop a crowd pushed and jostled to clamber onto the trackless trams, struggling against the passengers fighting to alight. Along the pavements little knots of youths lounged in twos and threes or more, watching the crowds streaming by, jeering, smoking, joking against the noise, under the balconies, in doorways, around the plate-glass windows. A half-mile of sound and movement and signs, signs, signs: Coca-Cola, Sale Now On, Jewellers, The Modern Outfitters, If You Don't Eat Here We'll Both Starve, Grand Picnic to Paradise Valley Luxury Buses, Teas, Coffee, Smoke, Have You Tried Our Milk Shakes, Billiard Club, The Rockingham Arms, Chine . . . nce In Korea, Your Recommendation Is Our Advert, Dress Salon.

Michael Adonis moved idly along the pavement through the stream of people unwinding like a spool up the street. A music shop was playing shrill and noisy, 'Some of these days, you gonna miss me honey'; music from across the Atlantic, shipped in flat shellac discs to pound its jazz through the loudspeaker over the doorway.

He stopped outside the big plate window, looking in at the rows of guitars, banjoes, mandolins, the displayed gramophone parts, guitar picks, strings, electric irons, plugs, jews-harps, adaptors, celluloid dolls all the way from Japan, and the pictures of angels and Christ with a crown of thorns and drops of blood like lipstick marks on his pink forehead.

A fat man came out of the shop, his cheeks smooth and shiny with health, and said, 'You like to buy something, sir?'

'No man,' Michael Adonis said and spun his cigarette-end into the street where a couple of snot-nosed boys in ragged shirts and horny feet scrambled for it, pushing each other as they struggled to claim a few puffs.

Somebody said, 'Hoit, Mikey,' and he turned and saw the wreck of a youth who had fallen in beside him.

'Hullo, Joe.'

Joe was short and his face had an ageless quality about it under the grime, like something valuable forgotten in a junk shop. He had the soft brown eyes of a dog, and he smelled of a mixture of sweat, slept-in clothes and seaweed. His trousers had gone at the cuffs and knees, the rents held together with pins and pieces of string, and so stained and spotted that the original colour could not have been guessed at. Over the trousers he wore an ancient raincoat that reached almost to his ankles, the sleeves torn loose at the shoulders, the body hanging in ribbons, the front pinned together over his filthy vest. His shoes were worn beyond recognition.

Nobody knew where Joe came from, or anything about him. He just seemed to have happened, appearing in the District like a cockroach emerging through a floorboard. Most of the time he wandered around the harbour gathering fish discarded by fishermen and anglers, or along the beaches of the coast, picking limpets and mussels. He had a strange passion for things that came from the sea.

'How you, Joe?' Michael Adonis asked.

'Okay, Mikey.'

'What you been doing today?'

'Just strolling around the docks. York Castle came in this afternoon.'

'Ja?'

'You like mussels, Mikey? I'll bring you some.'

'That's fine, Joe.'

'I got a big starfish out on the beach yesterday. One big, big one. It was dead and stank.'

'Well, it's a good job you didn't bring it into town. City Council would be on your neck.'

'I hear they're going to make the beaches so only white people can go there,' Joe said.

'Ja. Read it in the papers. Damn sonsabitches.'

'It's going to get so's nobody can go nowhere.'

'I reckon so,' Michael Adonis said.

They were some way up the street now and outside the Queen Victoria. Michael Adonis said, 'You like a drink, Joe?' although he knew that the boy did not drink.

'No thanks, Mikey.'

'Well, so long.'

'So long, man.'

'You eat already?'

'Well . . . no . . . not yet,' Joe said, smiling humbly and shyly, moving his broken shoes gently on the rough cracked paving.

'Okay, here's a bob. Get yourself something. Parcel of fish and some chips.'

'Thanks, Mikey.'

'Okay. So long, Joe.'

'See you again.'

'Don't forget the mussels,' Michael Adonis said after him, knowing that Joe would forget anyway.

'I'll bring them,' Joe said, smiling back and raising his hand in a salute. He seemed to sense the other young man's doubt of his memory, and added a little fiercely, 'I won't forget. You'll see. I won't forget.'

Then he went up the street, trailing his tattered raincoat behind him like a sword-slashed, bullet-ripped banner just rescued from a battle.

Michael Adonis turned towards the pub and saw the two policemen coming towards him. They came down the pavement in their flat caps, khaki shirts and pants, their gun harness shiny with polish, and the holstered pistols heavy at their waists. They had hard, frozen faces as if carved out of pink ice, and hard, dispassionate eyes, hard and bright as pieces of blue glass. They strolled slowly and determinedly side by side, without moving off their course, cutting a path through the stream on the pavement like destroyers at sea.

They came on and Michael Adonis turned aside to avoid them, but they had him penned in with a casual, easy, skilful flanking manœuvre before he could escape.

'*Waar loop jy rond, jong?* Where are you walking around, man?' The voice was hard and flat as the snap of a steel spring, and the one who spoke had hard, thin, chapped lips and a faint blonde down above them. He had flat cheekbones, pink-white, and thick, red-gold eyebrows and pale lashes. His chin was long and cleft and there was a small pimple beginning to form on one side of it, making a reddish dot against the pale skin.

'Going home,' Michael Adonis said, looking at the buckle of this policeman's belt. You learned from experience to gaze at some spot on their uniforms, the button of a pocket, or the bright smoothness of their Sam Browne belts, but never into their eyes, for that would be taken as an affront by them. It was only the very brave, or the very stupid, who dared look straight into the law's eyes, to challenge them or to question their authority.

The second policeman stuck his thumbs in his gun-belt and smiled distantly and faintly. It was more a slight movement of his lips, rather than a smile. The backs of his hands where they dropped over the leather of the belt were broad and white, and the outlines of the veins were pale blue under the skin, the skin covered with a field of tiny, slanting ginger-coloured hair. His fingers were thick and the knuckles big and creased and pink, the nails shiny and healthy and carefully kept.

This policeman asked in a heavy, brutal voice, 'Where's your dagga?'

'I don't smoke it.'

'Jong, turn out your pockets,' the first one ordered. 'Hurry up.'

Michael Adonis began to empty his pockets slowly, without looking up at them and thinking, with each movement, You mucking boers, you mucking boers. Some people stopped and looked and hurried on as the policemen turned the cold blue light of their eyes upon them. Michael Adonis showed them his crumbled and partly used packet of cigarettes, the money he had left over from his pay, a soiled handkerchief and an old piece of chewing gum covered with the grey fuzz from his pocket.

'Where did you steal the money?' The question was without humour, deadly serious, the voice topped with hardness like the surface of a file.

'Didn't steal it, baas (*you mucking boer*).'

'Well, muck off from the street. Don't let us find you standing around, you hear?'

'Yes, (*you mucking boer*).'

'Yes, what? Who are you talking to, man?'

'Yes, baas (*you mucking bastard boer with your mucking gun and your mucking bloody red head*).'

They pushed past him, one of them brushing him aside with an elbow and strolled on. He put the stuff back into his pockets. And deep down inside him the feeling of rage, frustration and violence swelled like a boil, knotted with pain.

THREE

Pushing open the swing doors with the advertisements for beer on each wing, Michael Adonis entered the pub, and inside the smell of wine and sawdust and cigarette smoke enveloped him. The place was just filling with the after-work crowd and the bar was lined with men, talking and drinking, and most of the table space was taken. Through a doorway to a back room he could see a darts game in progress. Somebody was saying, '. . . So I reckon to him, no, man, I don't fall for that joke . . .' Michael Adonis moved over to the bar and found a place between a stout man in a shabby brown suit, and a man with a haggard, wine-soaked, ravaged face. Around him the blurred mutter of conversation went on, then swelling when an argument over a big fight or a football game provoked a little heat.

The pub, like pubs all over the world, was a place for debate and discussion, for the exchange of views and opinions, for argument and for the working out of problems. It was a forum, a parliament, a fountain of wisdom and a cesspool of nonsense, it was a centre for the lost and the despairing, where cowards absorbed dutch courage out of small glasses and leaned against the shiny, scratched and polished mahogany counter for support against the crushing burdens of insignificant lives. Where the disillusioned gained temporary hope, where acts of kindness were considered and murders planned.

There were two Coloured youths in alpaca jackets and a balding Jew called Mister Ike serving behind the bar. He greeted every customer with a phlegmatic geniality which inspired a sort of servile familiarity.

One of the youths behind the bar came down from serving somebody and said, 'Hullo, Mike.'

'Hullo, Smiling.'

The haggard man looked sideways at him and said, 'Hallo, Mike . . .' But Michael Adonis did not return the greeting.

'Half white,' he said to the young bar-tender. While he was waiting for the tumbler of wine he lighted a cigarette, leaning on top of the bar, one foot on the rail over the trough on the floor. His mind switched back to the incident with the police, and then further back to the works' foreman with whom he had had the argument resulting in him losing his job, and he thought with rage, Effing sonofabitches.

The man in the brown suit looked his way and asked, 'What came today? You know?'

'*Weet'ie*. Don't know.'

'Number eighteen,' the haggard man said.

'Jesus. Had two bob on nineteen. Hell, and I even dreamed about eighteen last night. But thought I'd better play nineteen.' He began to recite the details of his dream, but nobody seemed to be listening.

Michael Adonis took a sip at his glass and felt the sweet wine warm his inside all the way down. Then he drank the rest in one swallow and took in the pleasant, spreading, slightly sour warmth that spread out over the walls of his stomach and then drifted gradually to his head. He ordered another half-pint and let it stand for a while, feeling the rage subside, looking at himself in the mirror behind the bar and saying in his mind to the young, tan-coloured, dark-eyed face with the new stubble and the cigarette dangling from the lips, Okay, trouble-shooter. You're a mighty tough hombre. Fastest man in Tuscon, until he saw the swing doors behind him open and Foxy and the two youths in the tropical suits come in to wipe the fantasy away.

They looked around and seeing him, came over.

'You seen Sockies, already?' the scarfaced boy asked.

'Nay, man.'

'*Hy is nie hier nie*. He isn't here,' Foxy said, looking around. 'Come, we blow.'

'Tell him we're looking for him, will you?' the scarfaced boy said. He had been smoking dagga and his eyeballs were yellow, the pupils dilated.

'Okay.'

They went out again, leaving the doors swinging and the man in the brown suit said, 'Those are hardcase lighties.'

'Seen them hanging around the Steps,' the haggard man, whose name was Mister Greene, said. 'That boy with the mark on his face, he was in reformatory last year. I know his people. Hendricks. Used to live up there in Chapel Street.'

'Bet they're out onto something.'

'They're just looking for one of their pals,' Michael Adonis told them.

'Fellow by the name of Socks.'

'No, jong. I don't like those boys.'

Michael Adonis picked up his drink and finished it, feeling the wine explode inside him and bring on a sudden giddiness. He stood against the bar, waiting for the nausea to pass, and then lighted another cigarette. The haggard man had been drinking gin and limejuice all the time and he was beginning to talk thickly. He belched loudly and swallowed.

'Hey, take it easy,' Michael Adonis said angrily to him. 'You'll mess up the whole blerry place.'

Greene hiccoughed and mumbled, 'Sorry,' wiping his mouth on a dirty handkerchief.

The pub was filling up and the tobacco smoke hung in a grey undulating haze, so that at the far end of the room the men took on the vague forms of wraiths in a morning mist; and the voices merged into a solid blur of sound. The doors kept swinging back and forth as men moved in and out. Outside the sun had gone and the lights had come on inside the bar and in shop-windows and box signs along the street. Glasses clink-clinked against the background of noise.

A man in a wind-breaker and an oilskin peaked cap, with a taxi-driver's licence badge pinned to the side of it, came in and pressed himself into the place between Michael Adonis and Greene. Under the cap he had a wily, grinning face and eyes as brown and alert as cockroaches. He grinned at Michael Adonis, showing tobacco-stained teeth and said:

'Howsit, Mikey?'

'Okay, how's business?'

'Not so bad. American ship came in this morning. Been driving those Yankees almost all day. Mostly to whore houses. Those johns are full of money. Just blowing it away on goosies.'

'Ya. Wish I could get a job on a boat,' Michael Adonis said. 'Go to the States, maybe.'

'Must be smart over there. You can go into any night-club and dance with white geese. There's mos no colour bar.'

The haggard man, Greene, hiccoughed and chipped in, saying, 'I read how they hanged up a negro in the street in America. Whites done it.'

'Huh?' Michael Adonis said.

'Read it in the paper the other day. Some whites took a negro out in the street and hanged him up. They said he did look properly at some woman.'

'Well, the negroes isn't like us,' Michael Adonis said. He thought about the foreman, Scofield, and the police, and the little knot of rage reformed inside him again like the quickening of the embryo in the womb, and he added with a sudden viciousness: 'Anyway those whites are better than ours, I bet you.'

'They all the same all over,' the taxi-driver said, swallowing his drink and lighting a cigarette.

'I don't give a damn for a bastard white arse,' Michael Adonis said and stared morosely into his glass.

'That's politics,' Greene said. 'Cut out politics.' He was a little drunk.

'It's the capitalis' system,' the taxi-driver said. 'Heard it at a meeting on the Parade. Whites act like that because of the capitalis' system.'

'What the hell do you mean—capitalis' system?' Michael Adonis asked. 'What's this capitalis' system you talking about?'

'I can't explain it right, you know, hey,' the taxi-driver answered, frowning. 'But I heard some johns on the Parade talking about it. Said colour bar was because of the system.'

'Shit.'

'Cut out politics,' Greene said again. 'Those bastards all come from Russia.' He hiccoughed again, spraying saliva from his slack mouth.

'What's wrong with Russia?' the taxi-driver asked. 'What you know about Russia?'

'Have a drink and cut out politics,' Greene said.

The taxi-driver said crossly: 'Look, old dad. If you don't know what you talking about, then hold your jaw.'

'Okay mate, okay,' Greene replied, grinning sheepishly. 'But it's true what I said about that negro in the States.'

'Man, that's muck all,' the taxi-driver said. 'I seen somebody killed in the street, too. I remember the time,' he started narrating, 'I saw Flippy Isaacs get cut up. You remember Flippy? He was in for housebreak and theff. Got two years. Well,' he went on, 'while Flippy is up at the oubaas he gets word that his goose is jolling with Cully Richards. You remember Cully? He mos used to work down here in Hanover Street at that butcher-shop. Amin's butcher-shop, man. Well, while he's in the big-house Flippy gets to hearing about Cully messing around with his goose. Well, ou Flippy didn't like that. Man, that john was a bastard of a hardcase. Further, he gets blerry wild when he hears about Cully and his goose. Further, when he comes out he just collects his gear and walks straight down to Hanover and calls Cully out of the butcher-shop. Cully comes mos out and Flippy says to him: 'I hear you been messing with my goose, hey? You been have a good time with my goose, hey? Cully doesn't say nothing but just stands there looking at him. Cully was a pretty tough juba himself. He just stands there looking at Flippy, dead pan. That makes Flip even wilder and he pulls out a knife. Don't know where he got it, but it was only a pen-knife.

'Well, when he pulls that knife Cully sees red and he runs back into the butcher-shop and gets a butcher-knife. A helluva long knife. Just so long.' The taxi-driver indicated the size of the knife, holding the palms of his hands apart in front of himself. 'Well,' he went on, 'Cully comes running out of the shop, his face all screwed up with rage, and goes for Flippy. Just one cut with that knife, man. It must have been about a foot long and sharp like a razor. You know those butcher-knives, man. Just one cut, jong. Across the belly. Right through his shirt. Hell, ou Flippy just sat down on the pavement and held his stomach, with his guts all trying to come out between his fingers, and the blood running down into the gutter. His whole face was blue. He just sat there, trying to keep his guts in.'

The taxi-driver took a sip at his drink to wet his throat, and continued. 'I think ou Cully must've got a shock. I don't think he mean to do it. But Flip pulling that knife made him mad. Even if it was just a small knife. Anyway, he looked blerry sick himself. He took one look at Flippy sitting there trying to hold his guts in and it coming out all the time. And Cully sits down next to him and tries to help him push his guts back. Sitting there and shaking and trying to push Flippy's guts back like somebody trying to put back a lot of washing that had fallen out of a bundle. You should've seen the people. Anyway, somebody called the ambulance, and the law came along, too. Flippy was about dead when the ambulance took him away. Ou Cully didn't say a word. Just stood there while the law handcuff him and put him in the van. He got five years, I think.'

'That isn't like whites hanging a negroo up,' Greene said, when the taxi-driver had finished his story. 'What's that got to do with whites hanging a negroo up?'

'Awright, wise guy,' the taxi-driver told him. 'You know a lot.'

'No, I don't know a lot. But what's that got to do with hanging a negroo up in the street?' Greene had been drinking while the taxi-driver had been talking and he had grown steadily drunk. 'What's that got to do with hanging a negroo up in the street?'

'Ah, shut up,' the taxi-driver said and turned away.

'Well,' Michael Adonis said, 'if anybody messed around with my goose I'd give him the same.'

'Me go to jail for a toit?' the taxi-driver scowled. 'Never.'

'A man's a man,' Michael Adonis told him. He was a little drunk too, and full of the courage of four glasses of wine. 'What good's a john if he let some other bastard steal his goose?'

'You'se be-effed,' the taxi-driver said. 'Anyway, I've got to blow!' He took his cap off and looked inside it and put it on again, adjusting it carefully, examining himself in the mirror behind the bar. 'Well, okay, pally.'

'Okay,' Michael Adonis said. His head was muzzy and there was a slight feeling of nausea in his stomach. He watched the taxi-driver go out, the swing doors flapped and then swung gently. A car went up the street, its engine revving and the tyres hissing on the asphalt. Michael Adonis turned and leaned on the bar and jerked his head at Smiling, the young barman. He ordered another pint of white wine and drank it down in two swallows, choking a little on the second, recovering and feeling the nausea replaced by a pleasant heady warmth. He put the glass down on the bar and lit another cigarette, then pulled himself out of the line. He picked his way through the press in the bar-room, through the smoke and liquor-smell laden atmosphere, and pushed through the swing doors.

FOUR

The air outside caught him suddenly in its cool grasp, making his skin prickle; and the glare of street-lights and windows made his head reel, so that he had to stand still for a moment to let the spinning of his brain subside. The spell of dizziness settled slowly, his head swinging gently back to normal like a merry-go-round slowing down and finally stopping. On each side of him the lights and neon signs stretched away with the blaze and glitter of a string of cheap, gaudy jewellery. A man brushed past him and went into the pub, the doors flap-flapping and the murmur of voices from inside had the sound of surf breaking on a beach. A slight breeze had sprung up over the city, moving the hanging signs, and scuttling bits of paper were grey ghosts in the yellow electric light along the street. There were people up and down, walking, looking into the shop-windows or waiting aimlessly.

Michael Adonis pulled up the zipper of his leather coat and dug his hands into the slanted pockets and crossed the street. The courage of liquor made his thoughts brave. He thought, 'To hell with them. I'm not scared of them. Ou Scofield and the law and the whole effing lot of them. Bastards. To hell with them.' He was also feeling a little morose and the bravery gave way to self-pity, like an advert on the screen being replaced by another slide.

He turned down another street, away from the artificial glare of Hanover, between stretches of damp, battered houses with their broken-ribs of front-railings; cracked walls and high tenements that rose like the left-overs of a bombed area in the twilight; vacant lots and weed-grown patches where houses had once stood; and deep doorways resembling the entrances to deserted castles. There were children playing in the street, darting among the overflowing dustbins and shooting at each other with wooden guns. In some of the doorways people sat or stood, murmuring idly in the fast-fading light like wasted ghosts in a plague-ridden city.

Foxy and the two youths in tropical suits stood in the lamplight on a corner down the street. They were smoking and one of them spun the end of his cigarette into the street. They watched Michael Adonis cross the street, but did not move from where they stood or say anything.

Michael Adonis turned into the entrance of a tall narrow tenement where he lived. Once, long ago, it had had a certain kind of dignity, almost beauty, but now the decorative Victorian plaster around the wide doorway was chipped and broken and blackened with generations of grime. The floor of the entrance was flagged with white and black slabs in the pattern of a draught-board, but the tramp of untold feet and the accumulation of dust and grease and ash had blurred the squares so that now it had taken on the appearance of a kind of loathsome skin disease. A row of dustbins lined one side of the entrance and exhaled the smell of rotten fruit, stale food, stagnant water and general decay. A cat, the colour of dishwater, was trying to paw the remains of a fishhead from one of the bins.

Michael Adonis paused in the entrance on the way to the stairs and watched the cat. It tugged and wrestled with the head which was weighed down by a pile of rubbish, a broken bottle and an old boot. He watched it and then reaching out with a foot upset the pile of rubbish onto the floor, freeing the fish head. The cat pulled it from the bin and it came away with a tangle of entrails. The cat began to drag it towards the doorway leaving a damp brown trail across the floor.

'Playing with cats?'

Michael Adonis looked around and up at the girl who had come down the stairs and was standing at the bend in the staircase.

'I'd rather play with you,' he said, grinning at her. 'Hullo, Hazel.'

'You reckon.'

She came down and stood on the first step, smiling at him and showing the gap in the top row of her teeth. She had a heavy mouth, smeared blood-red with greasy lipstick, so that it looked stark as a wound in her dark face. Her coarse wiry hair was tied at the back with a scrap of soiled ribbon in the parody of a pony-tail, and under the blouse and skirt her body was insignificant except for her small, jutting breasts. She was wearing new, yellow leather, flat-heeled pumps that gave the impression of something expensive abandoned on a junk heap.

Michael Adonis thought, Knockers like apples, and said, 'Where you off to, bokkie?'

'Bioscope. And who's your bokkie?' She peered at him, her eyes sceptical.

'Okay. Don't be like that. What's showing?'

'What's it now again? *Love Me Tonight*. At the Metro.'

'That's a nonsense piece. I went to the Lawn last night. *The Gunfighter*.'

'No what. That isn't nice. They tell me the boy dies at the end.'

'Ah, you girls just like them kissing plays.'

He reached into the pocket of the leather coat and got out the cigarettes, shook two loose and offered the packet to the girl. His hand shook a little and she looked at him, smiling, and saying, 'You've got a nice dop in, hey?'

'I got troubles,' he replied, scowling at her.

'You drowning your sorrows?'

'Maybe.' The mention of sorrows brought back the sense of persecution again and he surrendered himself to it, enjoying the deep self-pity for a while, thinking, I'll get even with them, the sonsabitches. They'll see.

The girl had taken a cigarette and he put the other between his lips, feeling for matches. He struck a light and held it to her cigarette, the flame wobbling between his fingers, and then lit his own.

The girl said, 'Well, I'm going to blow now.'

'Hell, wait a little longer. It's still early.'

'No, jong. I haven't booked.'

She edged past him, smiling, holding the cigarette between her lips with one hand in an exaggerated pose. He made a grab at her arm, but she skipped out of his reach, laughing, and darted out through the wide doorway, leaving him staring at it with a feeling of abandonment.

He said, aloud, 'Ah, hell,' and cursed, climbing the stairs and nursing the foetus of hatred inside his belly.

The staircase was worn and blackened, the old oak banister loose and scarred. Naked bulbs wherever the light sockets were in working order cast a pallid glare over parts of the interior, lighting up the big patches of damp and mildew, and the maps of denuded sections on the walls. Somewhere upstairs a radio was playing Latin-American music, bongos and maracas throbbing softly through the smells of ancient cooking, urine, damp-rot and stale tobacco. A baby wailed with the tortured sound of gripe and malnutrition and a man's voice rose in hysterical laughter. Footsteps thudded and water rushed down a pipe in a muted roar.

From each landing a dim corridor lined with doors tunnelled towards a latrine that stood like a sentry box at its end, the floor in front of it soggy with spilled water. Michael Adonis climbed to the top floor and cigarettes and liquor made him pant a little. The radio was playing below him now, a crooner singing of lavender and shady avenues, and the child cried again and again.

The latrine at the end of the corridor opened and a man clawed his way out of it and began making his way towards one of the doors, holding onto the wall all the way and breathing hard with the sound of a saw cutting into wood. He was old and unsteady on his legs and hampered by his sagging trousers. His shirt was out dangling around him like a night-gown. He made his way slowly along the wall, like a great crab, breathing stertorously.

Michael Adonis stood at the head of the stairs and watched him for awhile, and then strolled forward. The old man heard his footsteps and looked up.

'Why, hallo, there, Michael, my boy,' the old man said in English, his voice high and cracked and breathless with age. In the light of the bulb in the ceiling his face looked yellowish-blue. The purple-veined, greyish skin had loosened all over it and sagged in blotched, puffy folds. With his sagging lower eyelids, revealing bloodshot rims, and the big, bulbous, red-veined nose that had once been aquiline, his face had the expression of a decrepit bloodhound. His head was almost bald, and wisps of dirty grey hair clung to the bony, pinkish skull like scrub clinging to eroded rock.

'How are you, Michael boy?'

'Okay,' Michael Adonis answered, staring sullenly at the old man.

This old man, who was an Irishman and who was dying of alcoholism, diabetes and old age, had once been an actor. He had performed in the theatres of Great Britain, South Africa and Australia, and had served in two wars. Now he was a deserted, abandoned ruin, destroyed by alcohol and something neither he nor Michael Adonis understood, waiting for death, trapped at the top of an old tenement, after the sweep of human affairs had passed over him and left him broken and helpless as wreckage disintegrating on a hostile beach.

'Give us a hand, Michael boy,' the old man panted. 'Give us a hand.'

'What's the matter?' Michael Adonis asked. 'You got to the can, you ought to be able to get back.'

'That's not polite, Michael. You're in a bad mood. Tell you what, we'll sit down in my room and have a drink. You'd like a drink, wouldn't you? I've got a bottle left. Old age pension yesterday.'

'I don't want to drink your wine,' Michael Adonis said. 'I got money to buy my own booze with.'

'Who's talking about money?' the old man wheezed. 'Money's all the trouble in the world. Come on, Michael boy. Come on. Give your uncle a hand.'

'Youse not my uncle either,' Michael Adonis said, but took the stick-thin arm and eased the old man ungently over to a doorway. 'I haven't got no white uncles.'

'Thanks. What's the difference? My wife, God bless her soul, was a Coloured lady. A fine one, too,' the old man said, reaching for the knob and opening the door. He was partly drunk and smelled of cheap wine, sweat, vomit and bad breath.

The room was as hot and airless as a newly-opened tomb, and there was an old iron bed against one wall, covered with unwashed bedding, and next to it a backless chair that served as a table on which stood a chipped ashtray full of cigarette butts and burnt matches, and a thick tumbler, sticky with the dregs of heavy red wine. A battered cupboard stood in a corner with a cracked, flyspotted mirror over it, and a small stack of dog-eared books gathering dust. In another corner an accumulation of empty wine bottles stood like packed skittles.

The old man struggled over to the bed and sank down on it, clawing at his sunken chest with bony, purple-nailed fingers and waited for his breath to come back.

Michael Adonis slouched over to the window and stared out through a gap in the dusty colourless curtain and the grimy panes. Beyond, the roofs of the city were sprawled in a jumble of dark, untidy patterns dotted with the scattered smudged blobs of yellow. Hanover Street made a crooked strip of misty light across the patch of District Six, and far off the cranes along the sea front stood starkly against the sky.

He turned away from the window, anger mixing with headiness of the liquor he had consumed and curdling into a sour knot of smouldering violence inside him. The old man was pouring wine into the sticky glass, the neck of the bottle rattling against the rim so that the red sloshed about and wet his knuckled fingers.

'There you are, Michael me boy,' he cackled, breathing hoarsely. 'Nothing like a bit of port to warm the cockles of your heart.'

He held the glass up, his hand shaking, slopping the liquor, and Michael Adonis took it from him with a sudden burst of viciousness and tossed the wine down, then flinging the glass back into the old man's lap. The thick, sweet wine nauseated him and he choked and fought to control his stomach, glaring at the wreck on the bed, until the wine settled and there was a new heat throbbing in his head.

'A bad mood,' the old man quavered, and poured himself a glassful. He drank it, the wine trickling down his stubbly chin, and gasped. He cocked his head at Michael Adonis and said: 'You shouldn't get cross over nothing. What's the matter with you?'

'Aw, go to buggery.'

'Now, now, that's no way to talk. We've all got our troubles.'

'Ya. Bloody troubles *you* got.'

'God bless my soul, I've got my troubles, too,' the old man said, with a sudden whine in his voice. 'Here I am and nobody to look after an old man.' Tears of remorse gathered in his pale, red-rimmed eyes, and he knuckled them with a tangled skein of dirty cord that was his hand. 'Look at me. I used to be something in my days. God bless my soul, I used to be something.'

Michael Adonis lit a cigarette and stood there looking at the old man through the spiral of smoke. He said: 'What the hell you crying about. You old white bastard, you got nothing to worry about.'

'Worry? Worry?' the old man whined. 'We all got something to worry about.' He mustered himself for a moment and shook a dried twig of a finger at Michael Adonis. 'We all got our cross to bear. What's my white got to do with it? Here I am, in shit street, and does my white help? I used to be an actor. God bless my soul, I toured England and Australia with Dame Clara Bright. A great lady. A great actress she was.' He began to weep, the tears spilling over the sagging rims of his eyes and he reached for the bottle again. 'We're like Hamlet's father's ghost. I played the ghost of Hamlet's father once. London it was.'

'You look like a blerry ghost, you spook,' Michael Adonis said bitterly. He jerked the bottle from the old man's hand and tipped it to his mouth and took a long swallow, gagging and then belching as he took the neck from his lips. His head spun and he wanted to retch.

The old man said: 'Don't finish the lot, boy. Leave some for old Uncle Doughty.' He reached frantically for the bottle, but Michael Adonis held it out of his reach, grinning and feeling pleasantly malicious.

'Want a dop, Uncle Doughty?'

'Oh, come on, man. Don't torment your old dad.'

'You old spook.'

'Give us a drink, give us a drink, sonny boy.'

'What was that you were saying about ghosts? I like ghost stories.' Michael Adonis grinned at him, feeling drunk. He waggled the bottle in front of the decayed ancient face with its purple veins, yellow teeth and slack mouth, and watched the tears gather again in the liquid eyes.

'I'll tell you what,' the old man whined hopefully. 'I'll recite for you. You should hear me. I used to be something in my days.' He cleared his throat of a knot of phlegm, choked and swallowed. He started: 'I . . . I am thy father's spirit; doomed for a certain term to walk the night . . .' He lost track, then mustered himself, waving his skeleton arms in dramatic gestures, and started again. 'I am thy father's spirit, doomed for a certain time to walk the night . . . and . . . and for the day confined to fast in fires, till the foul crimes done in my days of nature's . . . nature are burnt and purged away . . . But . . .' He broke off and grinned at Michael Adonis, and then eyed the bottle. 'That's us, us, Michael, my boy. Just ghosts, doomed to walk the night. Shakespeare.'

'Bull,' Michael Adonis said, and took another swallow at the bottle. 'Who's a blerry ghost?' He scowled at the old man through a haze of red that swam in front of his eyes like thick oozing paint, distorting the ancient face staring up at him.

'Michael, my boy. Spare a drop for your old uncle.'

'You old bastard,' Michael Adonis said angrily. 'Can't a boy have a bloody piss without getting kicked in the backside by a lot of effing law?'

'Now, now, Michael. I don't know what you're talking about, God bless my soul. You take care of that old port, my boy.'

The old man tried to get up and Michael Adonis said, 'Take your effing port,' and struck out at the bony, blotched, sprouting skull, holding the bottle by the neck so that the wine splashed over his hand. The old man made a small, honking, animal noise and dropped back on the bed.

FIVE

Somewhere below a chain was pulled with a distant clanging sound and water welled and gushed through pipes, the sound dying with a hiss. The faraway mutter of a radio played rhumba music.

Michael Adonis stared at the bluish, waxy face of the old man and it stared back at him, with the blank artificial eyes of a doll. He said, 'Jesus,' and turned quickly and vomited down the wall behind him, holding himself upright with the palms of his hands and feeling the sourness of liquor and partly-digested food in his mouth. He stood like that, shaking, until his stomach was empty. His wine-stained hand made a big reddish mark on the wall.

The bottle had dropped to his feet, cracked at the base.

He straightened, staggering with the sudden reeling of his head and then sobered with the shock. He stared back at the wreck on the bed and said, aloud, 'God, I didn't mean it. I didn't mean to kill the blerry old man.' He wiped his mouth on the back of his hand and tasted the wine on it, then rubbed it dry on the seat of his jeans. A flood of thoughts bubbled through his mind. There's going to be trouble. Didn't mean it. Better get out. The law don't like white people being finished off. Well, I didn't *mos* mean it. Better get out before somebody comes. I never been in here. He looked at the sprawled figure that looked like a blowndown scare-crow. Well, he didn't have no right living here with us Coloureds.

He shivered a little as if he was cold, and lurched over to the door, holding onto the wall with one hand. He turned the knob and opened, looking out. His own room was a little way down the corridor. From the well of the stairs sounds drifted up: the radio was playing a smooth string number now, somebody laughed and feet thudded, a woman started scolding and a man's voice yelled back at her until she quietened, far away the sound of traffic interjected.

Comes from helping people, Michael Adonis thought, as he stepped out into the deserted corridor. He shut the door behind him and then walked quickly towards his room, hurrying as if the old man's ghost was at his heels. He reached his door and slid into the room, shutting the door quickly behind him. His head hurt and there was a sour taste in his mouth.

SIX

Police Constable Raalt lounged in the corner of the driving cabin of the patrol van and half listened to the radio under the dashboard. A voice, distorted by the mechanism, was clacking away, reading out instructions in a monotone. The other half of Raalt's mind was thinking, I'm getting fed-up with all that nonsense, if she doesn't stop I'll do something serious.

The van was parked up a dark street and at the intersection at the end of it the flow of Hanover Street was like the opening of a cave. Raalt searched in the pocket of his tunic until he found a crumpled packet and drew out a cigarette. It was the last one and he crushed the packet into a ball in his thick hand and flicked it out through the window. He lighted the cigarette and drew on it and thought: Well, her mother warned me she was a no-good bitch, but I was silly enough to think nothing of it. She won't get away with it, though. The bitch. He was thinking about his wife and it angered him that she was the cause of such thoughts. He eased his gun harness and scratched himself through the front of his tunic. There was a button missing on the shirt underneath. He had wanted to sew on the button before coming on duty but had been late and had not had the time to do it. He sewed and mended his own clothes and often he had to do the housework, too, and that angered him further. His wife had been good-looking before they had been married but now she had gone to seed, and that irritated him, too. He sat in the corner of the van and nursed his anger.

The driver of the patrol wagon sat behind the wheel and listened intently to the radio. He had no other thoughts except for what was being broadcast, and seemed oblivious of Raalt who lounged beside him. This policeman was young and slightly nervous and very careful to do everything according to regulations. That was something that irritated Raalt, too, but he did not reveal it except for little demonstrations of scorn, like smoking on duty.

After a while the voice on the radio ceased and the driver straightened and said: 'I think we ought to resume our patrol. Don't you think we've been parked long enough?'

Raalt removed the cigarette from his mouth, yawned and said: 'Okay, man. If you're not bloody fed-up with riding around looking at these effing hotnot bastards, let's go.' He tried to speak casually, hiding his anger from the driver, but it was there, like hard steel under camouflage paint.

The driver trod on the starter and worked the gears and they pulled away from the kerb, heading towards the lighted end of the street.

SEVEN

The youth who was called Willieboy thought: I should've asked him for a couple of bob. Here I am right out of chink and he with the pay he just drew. Mikey's not cheap, he'll give some start. I need a stop badly.

He began to walk in the direction of where he knew Michael Adonis lived.

Foxy and the two youths stood in the light of a shop-window and saw Willieboy approaching. A trackless tram went past, hissing like escaping gas on the asphalt. The summer night was clear and warm, except for the thin breeze that carried a warning of a Southeaster. The boy with the skull-and-crossbones ring on his finger said, 'Man, we can't look for that bogger all bloody night.'

'He'll turn up,' Foxy said. 'We'll ask Willieboy here to look out for him.' They waited for Willieboy to come up and the boy with the skull-and-crossbones ring said, 'Hoit. You seen Sockies yet?'

'Nay, man,' Willieboy said.

'If you see him tell him we're looking for him. Say to him we will get him at the Club. He must wait us there.'

'Okay.'

The scarfaced boy said, speaking to Foxy and the other, 'Well, let's go up to the Club. We might as well stick around there.'

'Ja, let's stroll,' the boy with the skull-and-crossbones ring agreed. They waved hands at Willieboy and went on down the street.

Willieboy thought, going in the other direction, I should've bummed a stop off them. I feel like a stop. He thrust his hands into the pockets of his trousers and wandered, shoulders drooping, along the pavement.

He passed the lighted windows, the pyramids of fruit, the price tags, the dismembered dummies draped in dusty dresses. Window-shoppers peered in through the plate-glass, pointing and marking the surface with smudges, leaving galleries of finger-prints. In the darkened doorway of a tenement between a fruit shop and a shoe store a couple made love, their faces glued together, straining at each other in an embrace among the piled dirt-tins and abandoned banana crates.

In the entrance of the building where Michael Adonis lived a heavy, bloated man in a filthy singlet was trying to find his matches, searching through the pockets of his decrepit trousers. He gave up the search and looked at Willieboy mounting the two cracked steps.

'Give metchie, please.'

Willieboy paused and held out a box of matches. The man nodded thanks, struck one and held it in his cupped hands to the bedraggled stump of a cigarette between his chapped lips. He had a greyish, puffed skin under the charred stubble and he carried the smell of stale wine with him.

Somewhere up in the damp intestines of the tenement a radio was playing and Willieboy climbed up the worn, sticky staircase into a crescendo of boogie-woogie, past the stark corridors with their dead-ends of latrines staring back like hopeless futures.

The electric light on the last floor flickered but did not go out, clinging determinedly to life as if it refused to be overwhelmed by the decay spreading around it. Willieboy walked down the corridor in the struggling glow and reached the door of Michael Adonis's room. He tried the handle. It was locked and he rattled it calling out softly. Willieboy rattled the doorknob again and then scowled and turned away from the door. He walked a little way back towards the stairs. He thought, maybe this old poor white will part with some start. And he turned to the room of the old Irishman.

Tapping on the door he said, 'Hey, Mister Doughty,' speaking with his ear close to the panel of the door. When he received no reply he rapped a little louder, calling again. Then he turned the knob and looking in, looked into the dead blue-grey face of the old man, and it glared back at him, wide-eyed, the stained, carious teeth bared in a fixed grin, with the suddenness of a shot from a horror film.

EIGHT

On the floors of the tenements the grime collected quickly. A muddied sole of a shoe scuffed across the worn, splintery boards and left tiny embankments of dirt along the sides of the minute raised ridges of wood; or water was spilled or somebody urinated and left wet patches onto which the dust from the ceilings or the seams of clothes drifted and collected to leave dark patches as the moisture dried. A crumb fell or a drop of fat, and was ground underfoot, spread out to become a trap for the drifting dust that floated in invisible particles; the curve of a warped plank or the projections of a badly-made joint; the rosettes and bas-reliefs of Victorian plaster-work; the mortar that became damp and spongy when the rains came and then contracting and cracking with heat; all formed little traps for the dust. And in the dampness deadly life formed in decay and bacteria and mould, and in the heat and airlessness the rot appeared, too, so that things which once were whole or new withered or putrefied and the smells of their decay and putrefaction pervaded the tenements of the poor.

In the dark corners and the unseen crannies, in the fetid heat and slippery dampness the insects and vermin, maggots and slugs, 'roaches in shiny brown armour, spiders like tiny grey monsters carrying death under their minute feet or in the suckers, or rats with dusty black eyes with disease under the claws or in the fur, moved mysteriously.

In a room down the corridor Franky Lorenzo lay on his back on the iron bedstead and stared at the ceiling. The ceiling had been painted white once, a very long time ago, but now it was grey and the paint was cracked and peeling and fly-spotted over the grey. The boards had warped and contracted so that there were dark gaps between them through which dust filtered down into the room whenever anything moved on the roof of the building. There were small cobwebs in the corners of the room, too, against the cornice. But he did not see these things now, because he was tired and irritable and happy and worried, all at the same time.

He wore a singlet and a pair of old corduroys and the singlet was dark with sweat and dust, and the corduroys shiny with wear, and there was coal dust in the grooves where the furry cotton had not been worn away. He had an air of harassment about him, of too hard work and unpaid bills and sour babies. An old scar above his left eye made a white mark in his bristly brown face. He had received the scar in a fight many years ago, when a man had hit him with a bottle. Under the singlet he had a massive chest, covered with thick, wiry hair, and his arms were thick and corded with veins and muscles, and he had a thick, heavy neck. The lines in his face, around the mobile mouth, and under the dark, deep-socketed eyes were full of old coal dust which he had never succeeded in washing away, and the eyes themselves, under the overhang of frontal bone and eyebrows, were soft and bright and young, like those of a little boy. His hands, clasped behind his head now, were hard and horny and calloused from wielding a shovel, and there was a faint odour of stale sweat and tobacco about him.

His wife had, a few minutes earlier, announced that she was once more pregnant and he was trying to decide whether it was good news or bad.

Four of their children lay sleeping in the narrow single bed against the wall on the other side of the room. They slept under the one thread-bare, worn, sweaty blanket, fitted together like parts of a puzzle into the narrow sagging space, two at each end of the bed with their legs carefully arranged. In time they would turn and twist in their sleep and the legs would become entangled, or they would kick one another and wake up, complaining and whimpering. Now they slept, the two boys together, their mouths open, and the two girls, their stringy hair plaited into tight ropes, all the heads pressed into the coverless, partly disembowelled, greasy striped pillows.

The fifth child was on her mother's hip, sucking noisily from a ginger-beer bottle fitted with an ancient teat, drinking sugared water. Grace, Franky Lorenzo's wife, held the child straddled on her hip and hoped that it would not cry and disturb her husband. She had a young-old face to which the beauty of her youth still clung, although her body had become worn and thickened with regular childbirth. Her face had the boniness and grandeur of an ascetic saint, and her eyes were dark wells of sadness mixed with joy.

Franky Lorenzo thought, They say, mos, it's us poor people's riches. You got no food in your guts, and you got no food for your children, but you're rich with them. The rich people got money but they got one, two kids. They got enough to feed ten, twenty children and they only make one or two. We haven't got even enough for one kid and we make eight, nine—one a year. Jesus.

He said aloud, 'Again. For what you want to get that way?'

'Well, it isn't my fault,' she told him.

'No. It isn't your fault.'

'You talk like it's all my fault. Whose fault is it then?'

He sat up and shouted angrily, 'Christ, you could mos do something. Drink something for it. Pills.'

'Maybe you ought to stop thinking of your pleasure every blerry night,' she flared back.

'Well, I got a right. Don't I say?'

'Ja. That's all you think about. Your rights.'

She started to cry softly, hugging the child at her hip. The children on the bed woke up, stared out over the ragged edges of their blanket.

Franky sank back on the bed and stared at the ceiling again. He felt a little ashamed now, hearing her quiet sobbing, and he began to wish he could do something good and beautiful for her. He looked at her with his deep, soft eyes and wanted to say something kind, but he could not find the words, and rubbed the back of one hand across the back of his mouth instead. He had hurt her, he felt, and love suddenly welled up inside him and choked his throat. He was tired, he thought. That made him angry. He was a stevedore and worked like hell in the docks and he felt angry with himself, too, now.

His wife sat down on a chair and looked at him and saw him only in a blur of tears and her own love beat like a pulse inside her.

She said huskily, 'Franky . . .'

From the bed Franky Lorenzo's voice held a gentle quality: 'Awright. It's awright. I'm sorry I shouted.' He did not look at her, out of embarrassment.

'Really, Franky?'

'Ja. Really.' He coughed, as if something was obstructing his throat, and said again, 'It's awright, woman. It's okay. Yes. Everything's okay.' Then with forced brusqueness: 'How about some tea, huh?'

'You . . . you hold the baby?'

'Of course. Why not?'

There was a table between the beds covered with newspapers, the edges cut into a frieze, on which were the kitchen things, and a primus stove. She picked up a saucepan and went out of the room to fill it at the tap in the latrine, while Franky Lorenzo held the child beside him on the bed.

NINE

Willieboy slammed the room door shut. A shout of fright rattled in his throat and he stood stock still for a moment, his face twitching with shock.

In that same moment a woman came out of the room opposite that of Michael Adonis. She was holding a saucepan in one hand and she had a young-old face and the body that bore the signs of regular childbirth. She stared at Willieboy sharply and said: 'Here, what you doing there?'

Willieboy turned quickly in panic, bolting for the head of the stairs and was gone down them, taking the steps three at a time, blundering into the banisters at the angle of each landing, while the woman reached the old man's door.

She rapped on the panels, calling out, 'Uncle Doughty, Uncle Doughty,' and receiving no reply turned the handle and looked in. She dropped the saucepan and her scream of terror reached Willie-boy as he cleared the last steps of the staircase.

In the lobby he crashed into the bloated man to whom he had given a match, sending him staggering and cursing, and then was out past the piled-up dust-bins, running up the street in the lamp-lit darkness.

It's enough to make a man commit murder, Constable Raalt told himself, sitting in the driving cabin of the patrol van. I'd wring her bloody neck but it's a sin to kill your wife. It's a sin the way she carries on, too. If I ever find out something definite she'll know all about it.

He glanced sideways at the driver beside him. The driver had a young face with plump, girlish jowls and light brown eyes. He was nervous of Raalt and perhaps a little afraid, although he tried now and then to break down the barrier it formed between them by attempting to be as co-operative as possible. Now he said, trying to make conversation: 'Things are quiet to-night, ne?'

'Quiet,' Raalt answered with a small sneer. 'I wish something would happen. I'd like to lay my hands on one of those bushman bastards and wring his bloody neck.' He found little relief in transferring his rage to some other unknown victim, but he took pleasure in the vindictiveness and his manner increased the discomfort of the driver who did not know what it was all about, but only sensed the rage that was consuming his companion.

He said: 'Well, the quieter the better. I don't like any trouble. Anyway, let these hottentots kill each other off for all I care. I want to get through this patrol and go home.'

They cruised down a dark street past leprous rows of houses, an all-night delicatessen making a pallid splash of light against the gloom, bumped over cobblestones, and swung into the garish strip of Hanover Street. The driver was turning over in his mind the idea of requesting a transfer to another station, anywhere else, as long as he would be away from Raalt. He did not like Raalt. He was becoming convinced of that. There was something about Raalt that increased his nervousness all the time they were together, so that it mounted at times almost to the point of fear. The driver was young and perhaps over-conscientious of his status both in the police force and in society, and he thought, He is one of those who will disgrace us whites. In his scorn for the hottentots and kaffirs he is exposing the whole race to shame. He will do something violent to one of those black bastards and as a result our superiority will suffer. They ought to post him somewhere, in a white area, where he will have little opportunity of doing anything dishonourable.

'Stop here,' Raalt said and the driver eased his foot from the accelerator so that the van slowed down and stopped by the curb side. The driver looked out and saw that they were outside a shuttered drapery.

Raalt climbed out without a word and slammed the door, and then, looking into the cabin, his eyes in the shadow with his back to the street-light, their irises hard and shiny as plate-glass, said: 'Hang on for me, *kerel.*'

The driver said: 'Okay, man,' and moving over looked out and back to watch Raalt go a little way down the pavement to where a sign over a door next to a darkened shop said: Jolly Boys Social Club. He thought, I wonder what rule he is going to break now.

Constable Raalt pushed open the street door and climbed a flight of chipped cement steps littered with cigarette butts, burned out matches and rubbish left by the nebulous community of loungers and hangers-on who frequented the club upstairs. At the top of the steps was a blistered brown door. Raalt tried the handle, found it locked and slapped the panels hard with the flat of his hand.

In the narrow dusty room beyond the door two men played snooker on the green table under the big shaded lamp and at another table a crowd threw dice, watching intently as the bone cubes sprang and bounced against the raised sides of the table, while at a third a quartet played cards with silent concentration. From the walls film stars stared down or away in various poses and a big blonde, wearing very few clothes, smiled toothily from under the cracked gloss surface of the picture. A painted sign pleaded vainly for the patrons to use the ashtrays since the floor was fed up; and smoke, laden with the tang of dagga, hung like a fog so that one could become pleasantly doped by merely drawing a few deep breaths.

When the banging of Raalt's hand on the door came to them the players in the room raised their heads, their eyes turned to where the sound came from, alert as foxes catching the scent of a hunter.

The two men at the snooker table stopped playing and rested on their cues, lighting cigarettes and blowing smoke casually in order to give the impression of nervelessness while a short, olive-skinned man in a once-white shirt and grey cardigan detached himself from the suspended dice game and made his way towards the door.

He had a round, flabby belly that protruded like a pregnancy over his belt, a round flat face and heavy grey lips with a fresh cigarette jutting at an angle from a corner of his mouth. The cigarette seemed to divide his face unequally on that side and on the other an old knife scar showed through the stubble on the cheek from the temple to the tip of his round chin, so that his whole face had the look of having been roughly split by a meat cleaver and then forgotten. His eyes were small and round and brown and flat and gritty as weathered sandstone under the blunt ridge of his forehead.

This man slid the bolt on the door and opened it a few inches, looking out, then stepped back, saying, 'Hullo, Boss Raalt,' as the constable pushed his way inside.

The silence hung now like armour-plate, hard and protective, and Raalt's smile was a crooked grimace, ugly as a razor slash. He shifted his grey-as-dust eyes onto the olive-skinned man who had shut the door now, and asked bitterly, 'How's business, Chips?'

'Slow, Boss Raalt, slow,' the olive-skinned man replied, the lids lowered like screens over the brown eyes, the cigarette jerking with each word.

'Take that cigarette out of your jaw when you talk to me,' Raalt said.

'Okay, Boss Raalt, okay,' Chips said and removed the cigarette, dropped it on the floor and put a wide foot on it. Under the lowered lids the eyes were hard and flat and shiny as the ends of cartridge shells, but the heavy grey mouth remained curled in the fixed smile.

He said to nobody in particular: 'Die baas Raalt, always making jokes. Always making jokes.'

Raalt held the dusty grey eyes on him and lifting his right hand up near his left shoulder struck the olive-skinned man across the mouth with the back of it, saying, spitting out each word: 'You don't have to smile at me, jong. I'm not your playmate.'

The olive-skinned man, Chips, stood quite still, only his head having jerked under the impact of the blow, with a faint stain of blood forming between the heavy grey lips, while behind him the people watched tautly in the smoke haze.

He said: 'Ja, baas,' speaking without humiliation, but with a heavy irony in his tone, and Raalt struck him again, so that the blood formed in a pool in the corner of his mouth and slid out and down that side of his chin in a thin, crooked trickle.

'You think mos you're a big shot,' Raalt said bitterly.

The olive-skinned man lifted a thick hand and wiped his mouth with it, looked at the bloodstain on the palm of his hand and then wiped it away slowly and deliberately on the leg of his stained trousers. He dug the same hand casually into the hip-pocket of the trousers and drew out a fistful of greasy crumpled notes. He counted off five pounds, put the rest away, and smoothed them carefully, arranging them with all their faces up, folded the sheaf neatly down the middle and passed it to Raalt. Raalt took it without a word and slipped it into the top pocket of his tunic, buttoning the flap down over it again, and gazed around at the silent men standing in the grey-smoke-filled room, then said: Well, you bastards are lucky I'm on this beat.' And to the man, Chips, he said, 'Don't do anything you don't want me to know about.'

The man made no reply, and Raalt asked, 'Do you hear me?'

'Ja, my baas,' smiling now thinly under the veiled, dark-copper eyes with the traces of blood beginning to congeal at the corner of his mouth and in the bristly stubble on his chin.

He held the door open and Raalt went by him and down the cement steps to the street. The olive-skinned man shut the door again, sliding the bolt carefully into place and then walked back to where the two men were chalking their cues again, not looking at him, and to where the crowd was gathering around the gambling table again, another man rattling the dice and saying, 'Come baby, make nick. Make nick.'

TEN

Michael Adonis lay on the iron bed in his dark room and heard the door-knob rattle. The room faced the street and from below the street-light made a pale white glow against the high window-panes and filtered a very little way into the gloom so that the unwashed curtains seemed to hang like ghosts in mid-air. The stained, papered walls were vague in the dark and the ceiling invisible. The door rattled again and somebody called softly outside in the corridor.

His flesh suddenly crawling as if he had been doused with cold water, Michael Adonis thought, Who the hell is that? Why the hell don't they go away. I'm not moving out of this place. It's got nothing to do with me. I didn't mean to kill that old bastard, did I? It can't be the law. They'd kick up hell and maybe break the door down. Why the hell don't they go away? Why don't they leave me alone? I mos want to be alone. To hell with all of them and that old man, too. What for did he want to go on living for, anyway. To hell with him and the lot of them. Maybe I ought to go and tell them. *Bedonerd.* You know what the law will do to you. They don't have any shit from us brown people. They'll hang you, as true as

God. Christ, we all got hanged long ago. What's the law for? To kick us poor brown bastards around. You think they're going to listen to your story; Jesus, and he was a white man, too. Well, what's he want to come and live here among us browns for? To hell with him. Well, I didn't mos mean to finish him. Awright, man, he's dead and you're alive. Stay alive. Ja, stay alive and get kicked under the arse until you're finished, too. Like they did with your job. To hell with them. The whole effing lot of them.

He shivered and fumbled around until he found a cigarette and lit it, the match flare lighting his face, revealing the curves of his cheekbones and throwing shadows into the hollows below them and around his eye-sockets. The rattling of the door-knob had stopped and he heard vaguely the sound of footsteps along the corridor. He puffed at the cigarette and blew smoke into the darkness.

You ought to get yourself a goose, he thought. You've been messing around too long. You ought to get married and have a family. Maybe you ought to try that goose you met downstairs. Her? *Bedonerd.* When I take a girl she's got to be nice. Pretty nice. With soft hair you can run your hands through and skin so you can feel how soft her cheeks are and you'd come home every night mos and she'd have your diet ready and Friday nights you'd hand over your pay packet and she'd give you your pocket money and you'd go down to the canteen and have a couple of drinks and if you got too fired up she'd take care of you. Funny how some rookers are always squealing about having to hand over their pay Friday nights. Jesus, if I had a wife I'd hand over my ching without any sighs. But she's got to be one of them nice geese, not too much nagging and willing to give a man his pleasure.

Then he sat bolt upright as a woman screamed in the corridor outside and the thought that jumped into his mind was, Oh, God, they found that old bastard. The woman screamed again and a door banged and a man began shouting and then some more doors were opening and banging, and feet pounded upstairs, along corridors, voices started speaking together. There was an uproar in the corridor outside and a man's voice said over and over, 'What the hell, what the hell, what the hell.'

Michael Adonis scrambled off the bed, the cigarette falling from his lips to the floor, sending off a shower of red sparks while he plunged towards the door. For a moment he was about to open it and dash out in his excitement, but he checked himself in time and clung to the handle, pressing himself against the woodwork, listening. He felt cold and shivery and then hot, and his mind raced.

There were several people in the corridor outside and above a hubbub of voices a woman was saying hysterically, '... old man. I saw who done it. I saw who done it. That skolly ...' A man's voice told her to shut up and Michael Adonis thought, How could she? She never saw a thing. We were all alone. There was nobody around. How could she have seen me? The bloody lying bitch. The bloody lying bitch.

The man started talking again and the hubbub ceased. '... better call the law ... No ... ambulance no use ... dead, isn't he? ... the law ... don't want no trouble ...' Somebody else said something and the man shouted, 'Christ, we leave it alone and the blerry law will grab the whole building on suspicion. Jesus, don't I know the law; I been in court four times all.'

Voices interjected, the man spoke again, his voice bearing a note of pride in his knowledge of the workings of the judiciary. Experience gave authority to his opinions. Conversation recommenced and the blur of voices rose, but without coherence in the room where Michael Adonis crouched. After a while it subsided to the muttering sound of distant breakers whispering against rocks, and then there was the sound of footsteps going downstairs, until the silence hung like a shroud on the upper floor of the tenement.

Michael Adonis released the door-knob and found the palm of his hand slippery with sweat. The liquor had gone from his brain now, and his mind was jumpy as a new-born child. He crossed over to the window, his heart beating hard, and stood by one side of the window peering down past the edge of the curtain. The street was quiet in the haze of the electric lights, the catacombs of darkened doorways beyond the grey pavements, and where lights were on in windows, they were yellow glows behind cut-out squares in black cardboard. Far beyond the rooftops of lower buildings neon signs cast a haze like a misplaced dawn over the city.

Then Michael Adonis saw the tenement crowd spill onto the pavement and into the street, eddying for a moment and then drawn in a small whirlpool around the vortex of a man in shirtsleeves and baggy grey flannel trousers. The light made a scar of the bald patch on his head and he waved his bared-to-the-elbow arms while he talked. The crowd stood around him, listening, and sometimes somebody said something, so that his arms and hands gestured again, as if he was making a speech. They went on talking for some minutes and after a while another man broke from the crowd and hurried up the street and into the dark.

Michael Adonis thought, coldly sober now. If they call the law they'll come up here sure and maybe want to know who lives here in these rooms. If they find me here then I'll go. I don't want no blerry questions asked. To hell with them. What's the bloody law done for them? Why, they can't have a little drink in and be found on the street without the law smacking them around. Christ, what a people. That smart son of a bitch down there who's doing all the talking is trying to be a laan, a big shot. What's it got to do with him? What'd that old bogger ever do for him? To hell with the lot of them. Stabbing a man in the back.

He watched the crowd in the street below for a while and then dropped the curtain and went back to the door. He turned the key and opened the door carefully. There was nobody out in the corridor. The old man's door looked stark and bare as a tombstone. Michael Adonis went out and shut the door quietly behind him. He walked carefully along the corridor and to the head of the stairs and looked down into the well. Somewhere the radio was still on, playing soft, syrupy music, all violins and horns. He went down the staircase slowly, listening all the time, until he reached the first landing, and then turned quickly towards the back of the building. A filthy window gave onto a low roof behind the tenement and below that into a squalid alleyway. Michael Adonis eased himself onto the roof which sheltered a disused boiler-house, and dropped down into the alley thick with accumulated muck. He ploughed his way towards the exit, stumbling over debris generations old and slimy with stagnant water, past dustbins and piled offal and into a side street. It was blocked at one end by a wall so that he had to walk towards the street where the crowd had gathered. They were a distance below the spot where he emerged and were talking together. He cut quickly out of the cul-de-sac and darted up the street away from the crowd.

A little way up the street Foxy and the two young men watched him go off into the darkness, and the scarfaced youth said: 'That looks like Mikey, don't I say?'

'Ja,' said Foxy non-committally. And to the boy with the skull-and-crossbones ring he said: 'Hey, go and find out what those jubas are gabbing about.'

The boy with the skull-and-crossbones ring sauntered off in the direction of the crowd in front of the tenement.

The scarfaced boy said: 'I wonder where in Jesus Sockies is. Looks like we get to search for him all blerry night.'

'He'll turn up,' Foxy said, not looking at him but at the crowd. 'I wonder what that is all about?'

ELEVEN

In the dark a scrap of cloud struggled along the edge of Table Mountain, clawed at the rocks for a foothold, was torn away by the breeze that came in from the south-east, and disappeared. In the hot tenements the people felt the breeze through the chinks and cracks of loose boarding and broken windows and stirred in their sweaty sleep. Those who could not sleep sat by the windows or in doorways and looked out towards the mountain beyond the roof-tops and searched for the sign of wind. The breeze carried the stale smells from passageway to passageway, from room to room, along lanes and back alleys, through the realms of the poor, until massed smells of stagnant water, cooking, rotting vegetables, oil, fish, damp plaster and timber, unwashed curtains, bodies and stairways, cheap perfume and incense, spices and half-washed kitchenware, urine, animals and dusty corners became one vast, anonymous odour, so widespread and all-embracing as to become unidentifiable, hardly noticeable by the initiated nostrils of the teeming, cramped world of poverty which it enveloped.

Willieboy strolled up the narrow back street in District Six, keeping instinctively to the shadows which were part of his own anonymity, and thought with sudden anger: Well, I had mos nothing to do with it. They can't say it's me. I found him mos like that. But years of treacherous experience and victimization through suspicion had rusted the armour of confidence, reduced him to the nondescript entity which made him easy prey to a life which specialized in finding scapegoats for anything that steered it from its dreary course. So that now he longed for the stimulants which would weld the seams of the broken armour and bring about the bravado that seemed necessary in the struggle to get back into the battle that was for hardened warriors only.

The look-out in front of the house halfway up an alleyway that was half stone steps and half cobbles was an old decrepit ghost of a man that sat in a ruined grass chair beside the doorway in the darkness of the high stoep facing the entrance of another street.

He saw Willieboy emerge from the lemon-coloured light of a street-lamp, recognized him, and relaxed, but maintaining an expression of officiousness with which he tried to hide his identity as another of the massed nonentities to which they both belonged. He nursed a sort of pride in his position as the look-out for a bawdy house, a position which raised him a dubious degree out of the morass into which the dependent poor had been trodden.

'Hoit,' Willieboy said, moving up the three steps onto the stoep.

An expressionless grunt, neither of welcome nor rejection, answered him. The old eyes were dull and damp as pieces of gravel in a gutter.

'Place open?'

'Ja,' the old man said reluctantly. 'Waiting for some sailors.'

He did not move as the boy turned to open the door. His business was to warn at the approach of enemies. He withdrew himself into the shelter of his own, old untidy thoughts as Willieboy went inside.

The front of the house was in darkness but beyond the dangling lace curtain at the end of the passageway light glared in the sitting-room. The floor was covered with bright linoleum decorated with geometrical designs, and there was a low table with a large clay vase containing coloured paper flowers held up in a piece of netting-wire. A big new radiogram stood against one wall and a sideboard displayed a pair of vases and a glass-covered tea tray with pictures of the Royal family behind the glass. The wallpaper was old, but there was still colour in the pattern of cabbage-like flowers and ribbons. A brocaded divan stood against another wall and its armchairs across two corners.

When Willieboy came into the room a woman stepped out of the kitchen. She was tall and big-boned and had a hard face with small dark eyes like two discoloured patches in brown sandstone. Her hair was tied back untidily into a bun and she wore two big gold rings in her ears. The rings were too big and did not suit her so that you noticed them all the time. Her mouth was crudely painted with bright lipstick. She was a lean, powerful woman with long arms, knobby wrists and big hands which displayed several rings.

The dark eyes looked suspiciously at Willieboy, and she asked sharply: 'Ja? And what do you want?'

Willieboy grinned at her, but under the harsh stare his bravado dwindled and he looked sheepish, saying: 'Hullo, Miss Gipsy. Miss Gipsy, I thought maybe you'd give us a little something on the book. You know, mos.' His hands came up, describing a bottle in the air.

'That'll be the day. You think I'm here to support all you bum-hangers?'

'Hell, come on, Miss Gipsy. I'll mos pay you soon as I get money.'

'Soon as you get money? You mean soon as you rob somebody again.'

'Come on, man, Miss Gipsy,' Willieboy said, whining a little. 'You know me, mos.'

'Well,' Gipsy said, 'Okay. But you don't pay up soon and you'll see.'

'Thanks, Miss Gipsy,' Willieboy smiled. 'You're real sporting.

The woman went back to the kitchen and Willieboy sat down on a chair. When Gipsy came back she brought a bottle of cheap wine which she put on the sideboard with a glass. She said: 'And don't sit here all night. I'm expecting some customers.'

'Okay, Miss Gipsy.'

Willieboy broke the seal of the bottle and poured the glass full. He emptied it at a swallow and felt the hot, raw liquor strike his stomach and burn for a moment before it spread out. It went to his head immediately and he felt a little dizzy, but after the second drink he settled into the sensation.

The woman did not come out of the kitchen again, and he drank on his own, taking his time and allowing himself to slip gently into a state of intoxication.

He had finished three-quarters of the bottle when there was a sound of a car pulling up outside, voices laughed and talked, and then the front door opened and people clattered into the passageway. The curtain parted and three men and three young women came in.

Two of the men were white, and the third was swarthy, with very black hair in shiny waves and a thin black moustache. One of the other men had red hair flowing back in a beautiful, natural pompadour. They all wore smart suits with loose draped backs and polo shirts.

One of the girls went over to the radio immediately and started a record. The dark seaman waited for her, while the other girls sat down on the divan with his companions.

A girl on the divan looked at Willieboy and said: 'How's it, pal?'

'Nice, Nancy, nice,' he said, smiling back at her. He did not look at the men, and thought lugubriously that she had no right to be there.

She was tan-coloured, and the bright dress she wore added something so that you had to look at her again, and then you saw that she was beautiful. There was beauty in the depths of her dark eyes and in the lines of tragedy around her mouth, in the lost youth of the used shape of her body.

'You look cross,' she said to Willieboy, and to the redheaded seaman, 'He's my old pally.'

The seaman said, 'Uh huh,' grinning.

Then the woman, Gipsy, sailed in from the kitchen and said loudly, smiling at them all: 'Hullo, gentlemen. See you brought my girls home.'

The seamen got up and shook her hand, and the dark one stopped dancing for a moment to do likewise. The girl with whom he was dancing said: 'Bring us a bottle of brandy, Gipsy.'

'Right away,' Gipsy said. She laughed and said to the men: 'Make yourselves at home, boys.'

The music stopped and the black-haired man released his partner, guiding her over to an armchair, saying something in Spanish that she did not understand, but which made her giggle. She sat down and crossed her legs and the seaman sat on the arm of the chair with one hand on her neck. Willieboy watched him sullenly.

Gipsy came back with brandy and glasses and poured a row of drinks. They all drank, clinking glasses, and the girls laughed breathlessly as the spirits went down. Willieboy thought, I bet she put tobacco in that stuff.

The redhead said to him: 'How about you, buster? Have a drink?'

Willieboy looked at him. The redhead seemed to waver and undulate before him, and he was feeling drunk. He said with dignity: 'I got my own, pal.' He reached for his bottle of cheap wine and poured a drink. His hands shook a little.

'You better go slow on that,' the girl, Nancy, said.

'I can take it,' Willieboy said thickly. 'What do you think I am? A squashie?'

'Man, you put that stuff down real solid,' the other man on the divan said patronizingly.

Willieboy looked at him sullenly and asked: 'Youse guys from the States?'

'Yeah, man,' the seaman said. 'This here's Red and mah name's George. Red here, he from Chicago, see. That's some burg, that is. You all heard abaht Chi, Ah guess.'

'Yes,' Willieboy said. 'Gangsters.'

'Yeah, man. That's raht, man. Nah me, Ahm from down Looziana way. That's dahn Sahth.'

'South America?'

'Naw, man. Ah mean the Sahthern part o' Northern 'Merica, see?'

Willieboy did not understand this and directed his attention at the Spanish-speaking one and asked: 'Who is he? Cesar Romero?'

The Spanish-speaking man looked up and across at him, frowning, and George laughed and said: 'Naw, he ain't Cesar Romero, that's Ray Ybarra. He's Puerto Rican, but comes from Noo York.'

'Ain't he American?' Willieboy asked, feeling confused and drunk.

'Of course he's American,' the girl with George said. 'Don't be so blerry stupid.'

They all laughed and Red hugged the girl, Nancy, to his body, and the Puerto Rican from New York began to fondle the girl in the armchair. They had some more drinks and then Gipsy came in again.

The men smiled at her and George said: 'Hallo, little girl.'

She grinned at him and said: 'You better treat my girls nice, hey?'

'Sure ma'am,' Red replied. He smiled at the girl, Nancy, and stroked her hair.

Willieboy was drunk and angry from being laughed at and now he said to the woman: 'Listen, Gipsy, what you let the girls mess with these boggers for? They foreigners.'

The woman, Gipsy, turned on him. 'You. What the hell you talking about?'

'These jubas. They just messing our girls.'

'That any of your business?'

'I don't like them messing our girls,' Willieboy said again, staring at the three men. 'To hell with them.'

'Leave him alone, Gipsy,' the girl, Nancy, said to the woman.

'You stick to your business,' Gipsy told her, and to Willieboy, 'And what right you got talking about my guests?'

'Guests—' Willieboy sneered, looking at the seamen and feeling angry. 'They got no right messing with our girls.'

The seamen were quiet now, looking at him. They could not understand what he was saying, but they sensed his antagonism.

Gipsy said: 'You got a cheek coming to drink on the book and then insulting my real customers.'

'Awright, I'll pay you for it. They can keep their blerry brandy too. I don't want their blerry brandy.'

'You keep quiet if you want to stay here,' Gipsy snapped at him. 'You don't know how to act in front of respectable people.'

'Awright, Gipsy,' Willieboy said and looked at the seamen. 'Let them mess with the girls.'

'Keep quiet, man,' Nancy told him, speaking kindly. 'It's all right, man. You just keep quiet. You want another drink?'

'No,' Willieboy said. 'Why don't you leave them, Nancy?'

'He's just a little drunk,' Nancy told Red. 'He don't mean nothing.'

'Why don't you throw him out, the unmannerly bogger,' the girl with the Puerto Rican said.

'Gwan,' Willieboy said to her. 'Who's you?'

The Puerto Rican seaman looked at him and said: 'Listen, don't talk to a lady like that.' He got up and went on looking at Willieboy.

George stood up, too, and said: 'Now, Ray. This don't call for no fight, boy.' And Gipsy said: 'I don't want trouble here. This is a respectable place.'

'Then tell him to lay off,' the Puerto Rican said. He looked mean and dangerous.

'Come on, get out,' Gipsy said to Willieboy. 'You drunk and you make trouble.'

Willieboy ignored her, but was looking at the seaman. He was still a little drunk and spoiling for a fight.

'Go, man, Willieboy,' Nancy said. 'Come around in the morning.'

'That juba got no right talking to me that way, mos,' Willieboy said, still looking at the seaman.

'You better go, kid,' the Puerto Rican told him.

Willieboy lunged at him suddenly and he stepped back startled, but Gipsy had her arms around Willieboy before he could do anything else. She was strong and she held onto him while Willieboy struggled. The girls began to scream and the two other seamen stepped forward. Willieboy suddenly went berserk and threw Gipsy from him with a savage twist, so that she staggered into the table upsetting it and scattering the glasses and the near-empty brandy-bottle.

'God, I'll chop you,' Willieboy shouted and reached for his jacket pocket.

'Watch out for his knife,' Gipsy shouted, and they saw the sharpened kitchen knife gripped in his hand.

'Willieboy. No, man,' the girl, Nancy, cried out.

The seaman whose name was George reached out, picked up the fallen brandy-bottle and flung it. He was drunk, too, and his aim was bad, so that it missed Willieboy by a yard and splintered against the wall somewhere, leaving a stain on the wallpaper. Willieboy swung at him with the knife, but his feet became entangled with the legs of the overturned table and he lurched, and at that moment Gipsy hit him expertly behind an ear. He fell on his face over the table, dropping the knife, and groaned.

The Puerto Rican seaman stepped forward and prepared to kick him in the head, but Gipsy said sharply: 'Don't do that. Leave him.' The Puerto Rican drew back, cursing in Spanish.

Meanwhile the front door had opened and the look-out came in, running down the passageway and saying: 'No man. No, man.' His mouth was open and his old eyes looked startled.

Gipsy looked at him and said derisively: 'A hell of a time for you to come.'

The old man looked at Willieboy who stirred in the wreckage of the table and broken glasses, and asked: 'What'd he do, Gipsy?'

'Ran amuck and tried to chop these visitors. You better put him out in the street.'

'Don't hurt him,' Nancy said.

'Garn,' Gipsy said to her. 'You talk like he was your man.'

'I know him a long time,' Nancy said. 'He is always so luff.'

Red put an arm around her and said: 'Now you all don't get excited, kid.'

The look-out got his hands under Willieboy's armpits and hauled him over, then started to drag him down the corridor to the front door. His heels made a squealing sound on the oilcloth. Gipsy stooped and picked up the fallen knife and placed it on the sideboard.

'He'll get into trouble over that knife, one day,' she said. 'Now you girls better clear up. These blerry skollies always making trouble for respectable people.'

'Put on the gram,' one of the girls said.

George laughed and said: 'That little scrap just give me a thirst. You reckon you can rassle up another bottle, ma'am?'

'Yes,' Gipsy said. 'That's another twenty-five bob.'

Outside the old man dumped Willieboy on the stoep. He was wheezing from dragging the limp youth, and he grumbled irritably:

'Always got to do the dirty work. Always doing the blerry dirty work.' Inside the radio began to play again.

Willieboy came to slowly and sat up, holding his head where Gipsy had hit him. He blinked at the look-out and asked angrily: 'You hit me, you effing bastard?'

'It must have been the woman,' the look-out said. 'She got a blow like the kick of a horse. I already seen her knock the front teeth out of a sailor once. You better go, pal.'

Willieboy looked at him for a moment, and then rolled over suddenly to the edge of the stoep and was sick onto the pavement. He lay there, panting for a while, after retching was over. Then he stood up and lurched down the steps and went down the street, walking unsteadily in the dark.

TWELVE

The driver saw the crowd first and said, bringing Constable Raalt out of his thoughts, 'What goes on here?'

He eased his foot on the accelerator bringing the patrol van slowly up to the crowd. Raalt had been thinking morosely about his wife again and the sight of the crowd pleased him a little with its relief from his gnawing thoughts. He was out on the running-board before the van came to a stop and his hard grey eyes swung over the crowd from face to face like the expressionless lenses of a camera.

The crowd was scattered from the entrance of the tenement, across the pavement in front of it and onto the street. Now, as the van pulled up, those in the street withdrew partially towards the edge of the pavement, faces passive and eyes downcast in the presence of the law. A few slid quietly away into the shadows beyond the lamp-light, for there was no desire in them to cooperate with these men who wore their guns like appendages of their bodies and whose faces had the hard metallic look, and whose hearts and guts were merely valves and wires which operated robots.

'Nou ja, what goes on?' Raalt's voice cracked out.

The crowd eddied and rippled for a few moments and then parted as a heavy, wine-bloated man pushed his way forward. 'What you scared of?' he muttered to all in general. 'Can't you blerry well talk?' He looked at Constable Raalt and grinned ingratiatingly. He said: 'There's a dead man upstairs. Look like murder, baas.'

Constable Raalt stared back at him and said: 'How the hell you know what's murder and what isn't, jong?'

The bloated man grinned again and moved his feet. He said: 'Well, Konstabel, I reckon I saw who did it.'

'Oh, you did? And what is your name, kerel?'

'John Abrahams, baas.'

Somebody in the crowd cried: 'Hey, jou fif' column,' and Raalt's flat grey eyes glanced around from face to face. The crowd muttered and shuffled again, and now their eyes were on Abrahams. He could feel hostility in the stares and he grinned sheepishly, but turned his head and said: 'Well, we must mos cooperate with the law, don't I say?'

'Ja,' another man said, looking at him and ignoring the police. 'Yes, cooperate like they did with Noortjie.'

'What of Noortjie?' Abrahams scowled.

'You know mos. Because he was a little drunk one night they took him to the cells and boggered hell out of him all night. Lost his teeth, and when he came in front of the court they said he'd resisted arrest and he got extra for that, too. Okay, cooperate with them, man.'

'Well, who told him to get drunk?' the puffy man asked. He turned back to Constable Raalt and said: 'Don't listen to them, baas. I believe in law and or'er.'

'Oh,' Constable Raalt said, smiling at him with a small sneer. 'You believe in law and order. That's very good, jong.' He looked at the driver and said: 'He believes in law and order.' To the man he said again: 'Good. Give us some of your law and order.'

Abrahams looked at his shoes and shuffled and smiled. 'Well, baas, I was standing there in the doorway and this rooker come along and I ask him for a match and he give me one to light my endtjie, my cigarette-end, then he go in upstairs and I stand but here all the time and the next thing I hear a woman screaming and this rooker come running down and almost run me over and I see him running up the street fast.' He paused for breath and continued, 'Further, I go upstairs, and the people here who live inside also go upstairs and there we see this old man dead.' He stopped and then looked about him with a sort of shabby pride. The people surrounding him stared back and he shook off their antagonism with a shrug and said again to Constable Raalt: 'You see how it is, baas? These people.'

Constable Raalt did not offer comment, but without turning his head, said to the driver: 'We'd better go in and look.' To the bloated man he said: 'You better come with us. The rest of you can eff off.'

He scattered the crowd as he walked through it to the entrance of the tenement, the driver following and Abrahams bringing up the rear. The throng closed again and some ventured in behind them, voices muttering that they lived here, anyhow.

Climbing the smelly staircase into the heights of the building, the driver thought, with disgust, that he did not mind if the whole population of this place killed themselves off as long as it was not done while he was on duty. This was a bloody nuisance, and he relegated them all to hell, including Constable Raalt. At the same time he was glad Raalt was with him, for he was new to the force and this district where the people had little regard for the authority of the land, and he was not sure that he would have been able to handle this thing, which seemed to be murder, too.

They reached the top floor and the driver felt trapped there by the smell of decay and disintegration. He heard Raalt snapping at the group that crowded behind them and somebody shuffled over to gesture at a door. The dim, half-burned-out bulb in the socket in the ceiling glowed weakly so that the shadows of the people were blurred and blotched.

He went behind Raalt into the room and the crowd behind tried to push in with them and he turned and shouted irritably: 'Listen here, muck off. Keep outside.'

The stench of vomit hit him with a sour blow and he stared at the bluish dead face of the old man on the bed. He said: 'Jesus Christ.'

Raalt went over and looked closely at the dead face, examining it without touching it. It was the first time he had looked at a corpse this way, but he tried to give the driver an impression of experience. He felt a little disgusted. He straightened up and said to the driver:

'Looks like he was hit on the head.'

'It's a job for the detectives,' the driver said, looking around with a grimace of nausea. 'I'll get the station on the wireless.'

'What's your hurry, man?' Constable Raalt asked. 'This is our patrol, isn't it?'

'Naturally. But it is a case for the criminal investigation volk,' the driver replied, without looking at him.

Raalt said: 'Nobody kills anybody on my beat and gets away with it. No bloody bastard.'

Looking again at the corpse, the driver said: 'A white man, too.

What would a white man be doing living in a place like this?' He looked away from the corpse and around the room, wrinkling his nose at the smell of vomit, wine, decay.

Raalt said nothing, but unbuttoned the flap of his pocket and took out his notebook. He glanced at his wristwatch and then began to write in the book. The driver said, a little impatiently: 'I had better get onto the wireless.'

Constable Raalt looked up at him from his writing with his hard grey eyes and then said, grinning: 'Very well. Get the station on your beautiful wireless and tell them to send the detectives. Also give them my greetings and best wishes. Also a blessed Christmas.'

The driver glanced at his eyes, shook his head and went out. Constable Raalt wrote again in his notebook and through the writing thought, I wonder what she's doing now, the verdomte bitch, I'll break her neck if I catch her at something. He finished writing and then went to the door of the room. He had become oblivious of the sour smell in the room and it was now merely a smell, like stale tobacco or the smell of disinfectant in the police station.

The people gathered in the corridor, near the upper landing, gazed back at the constable, some of them nervously, some with surreptitious boldness, all with the worn, brutalized, wasted, slum-scratched faces of the poor. They saw the flat grey eyes under the gingerish eyebrows, hard and expressionless as the end of pieces of lead pipe, pointed at them.

'Now,' he said coldly. 'Now, where is the woman who is supposed to have screamed?'

The people on the landing and in the corridor said nothing, looking away, and Constable Raalt thought, These bastards don't like us; they never did like us and we are only tolerated here; I bet there are some here who would like to stick a knife into me right now.

He said, sneering: 'What's the matter? She didn't do it, did she?'

The man, John Abrahams, laughed a little and said: 'They won't say a thing, baas. You know how it is.'

'No, I don't know how it is,' Raalt told him. 'You tell me how it is.'

'Well, baas . . .'

'All right, forget it, man. What's your name, anyway?'

'John Abrahams, Konstabel. I told baas.'

Raalt wrote it down in his notebook, together with the address. 'What is the name of the man inside?' Gesturing with his head towards the door of the room where the body lay.

'Mister Doughty,' the man Abrahams said.

'Doughty? What sort of a name is that? How do you spell it?'

'I don't know, baas. We just called him Mister Doughty.'

'Doughty,' Constable Raalt repeated. 'What a peculiar name. These people have bloody peculiar names.' Then he remembered that the body was that of a white man and he asked: 'What was he doing here? How did he get here?'

'He lived here a long time,' Abrahams replied. 'He got a pension and he was in the big war. I heard him talk about it once.' He added with a grin, 'Drank like hell, too.' He looked down at his feet when Raalt stared at him.

'Now,' Raalt said, when he had written down the old man's name in his notebook without bothering to try to spell it correctly: 'Tell me, how did this man look whom you saw running away.'

Before Abrahams could answer Franky Lorenzo said to him from the crowd in the corridor: 'You've said enough already, Johnny.'

Constable Raalt raised his head and looked at Franky Lorenzo, his grey eyes bleak. He said: 'Listen, jong, you seem to have a lot to say. You had a lot to say downstairs, too. Do you want to be arrested for intimidating a witness and defeating the ends of justice?'

Franky Lorenzo did not understand these high-sounding phrases but he sensed the threat. Still he met the constable's eyes holding them with his own, until he felt his wife tugging at his arm, pleading: 'Franky, don't get into trouble, please. Remember . . . remember . . .'

'All right,' Franky Lorenzo said sullenly. 'All right.' He looked across at Abrahams for a moment and then looked away again.

Constable Raalt said: 'Pasop,' to him and then to Abrahams: 'Now, then. Come on.'

'Well, baas,' Abrahams hesitated, feeling a little nervous and embarrassed now. 'Well, baas, you see I didn't execkly see . . .'

'Oh,' Constable Raalt said, his voice hard. 'You didn't exactly see. What exactly did you see?'

'Well, baas, he was just a boy. One of these young rookers that hang out on the corners. I can't say execkly . . .'

John Abrahams was now beginning to feel the effect of the abrasive stares of those around him and his bravado commenced to collapse, falling from him like dislodged coloured paper decorations. He shuffled and stared at his feet and fingered his nether lip, trying to salvage some of the disintegrating sense of importance.

'Listen, man,' Raalt told him. 'If you don't want to talk now you can still be forced to appear in court and say what you know before the magistrate. So make up your mind.'

John Abrahams collapsed completely and said quickly: 'He was just a young rooker, baas. He had on a yellow shirt and a sports coat and had kinky hair. That's all I seen, baas, true as God. That's all.' He looked around helplessly and cried out: 'Well, I got to tell what I saw, mustn't I?'

The crowd was silent and Constable Raalt, writing in his notebook again thought, They hate us, but I don't give a bloody hell about them, anyway; and no hotnot bastard gets away with murder on my patrol; yellow shirt and kinky hair; a real hotnot and I'll get him even if I have to gather in every black bastard wearing a yellow shirt.

He said, his grey eyes narrowed with rage: 'All right, the rest of you can bogger off. Abrahams, you stay here and wait for the detectives.'

'Can't I go, baas?' Abrahams asked, whining now.

'No, God, jong. I said wait for the detectives.'

He added to his thought, Detectives; I can look after my own troubles; that boy and his detectives.

He stared at the crowd in the corridor, his eyes like pieces of grey metal, and they started to disperse, slowly trickling away. Franky Lorenzo looked again at Abrahams and spat on the floor, then walked down the corridor with his wife. Constable Raalt returned his notebook to the pocket of his tunic and buttoned the flap. He waited for the detectives to arrive, and began to think again of his own wife.

THIRTEEN

Michael Adonis turned into the little Indian cafe and saw the boy, Joe, sitting at one of the baize-covered tables, eating. Michael Adonis had seen the cafe as he came into the short, grey, yellow-lamp-lighted street with its scarred walls and cracked pavements, and had headed towards it because he had been walking about for an hour and wanted to sit down. He saw the pale glow of the cafe light behind the greasy window piled with curry-balls and Indian sweetmeats and headed for it like a lost ship sighting a point of land for the first time after a long and hopeless voyage.

He parted the sparse wooden-bead curtains and saw Joe at the table. Behind a glass case full of stale rolls an old, bearded Indian dozed, his betel-stained mouth half-open and his beard stirring as he breathed. There was nobody else in the cafe.

Joe looked up as Michael Adonis came over, and smiled. He was eating curried peas and rice with one hand, arranging the food skilfully into a little mound and then shovelling it into his mouth with his grouped fingers. Some of the food had spilled onto his disreputable old raincoat, adding fresh stains to many others.

He said: 'Hey, Mikey. You out late.'

Michael Adonis sat down opposite him and said, scowling: 'Same with you. Where in hell do you live?'

Joe smiled, shrugging, and waved his free hand. The nails were rimmed with black, and the smell of fish still clung to him. 'Anywhere,' he said.

Then he added, still smiling, but a little shyly: 'Bought the curry with the shilling what you gave me. The old Moor sells shilling's worth.'

'I had supper,' Michael Adonis told him and lighted a cigarette. He smoked silently, brooding.

'What you walking about for, Mikey? You look sick, too.'

'I'm not sick. I got troubles.'

Just then the old Indian woke up and saw him, and came over, wiping his hands on his stained and greasy apron. 'You want eat?' he asked.

'No,' Michael Adonis said. 'Bring me some coffee.'

'No coffee. Tea.'

'Awright.'

The old Indian went over to the hatchway in the back wall and called through into the kitchen.

Michael Adonis got out his cigarettes and lit one, watching Joe eating the curry. Joe scooped some of the food into his mouth, chewed, the yellow gravy staining the outer corners of his lips. He said, philosophically: 'We have all got troubles. Don't I say?'

'You. Troubles,' Michael Adonis said, looking at him with some derision. 'What troubles you got?'

He was suddenly pleased and proud of his own predicament. He felt as if he was the only man who had ever killed another and thought himself a curiosity at which people should wonder. He longed to be questioned about it, about the way he had felt when he had done it, about the impulse that had caused him to take the life of another. But the difficulty was that to reveal his secret was dangerous, so he had to carry it with him for all time or accept the consequences. The rights and wrongs of the matter did not occur to him then. It was just something that, to himself, placed him above others, like a poor beggar who suddenly found himself the heir to vast riches. And the fact that he dared not declare his newly acquired status irritated him, too, so that now he felt a prick of jealousy for this nondescript boy who was in a position to disclose his own problems with ease if he wished to.

He said, surlily: 'Where the hell you get troubles from?'

But at that moment the bead curtains over the doorway of the cafe parted and Foxy and the two youths in their smart tropical suits came in. They saw Michael Adonis and Joe at the table and came over.

They looked with some disgust at the ragged boy and then immediately ignored him, and Foxy turned to Michael Adonis, saying: 'We still looking for that bastard Sockies. Did you see him yet?'

'No, man.'

The boy with the scarface spat on the floor and said: 'We walking around all night looking for that hound. We ought to find another look-out.'

'You feel like doing something with us?' Foxy asked Michael Adonis.

'What?'

'Leave him alone,' the boy with the skull-and-crossbones ring growled.

'We need a man to hold candle at a job,' Foxy replied, ignoring the youth. 'We'll give you a cut.'

'Who the hell is he?' the boy asked, looking at Michael Adonis scornfully.

I wonder how many people you killed, Michael Adonis thought with his distorted pride, staring back at the boy with the ring, a thin smile on his lips, and said: 'What do you know about me?'

The one with the scarface then said: 'Maybe he's okay.'

Foxy asked: 'You want to come in, Mikey?'

Michael Adonis looked again at the boy with the ring. 'What about him?'

'He's okay,' Foxy told him, grinning. 'He's just a little hardcase, that's all. But he's awright.'

'Well,' Michael Adonis considered, rubbing the faint stubble on his chin. 'Well, maybe. I don't know yet.' He felt a stir of pleasure at being approached, but he was still hesitant.

Foxy shrugged and said: 'We going down to the Club now. We not going to bogger around looking for Sockies no more. We'll be down at the Club, so get us there when you make up your mind.' He added: 'You could make some chink now you haven't got a job no more. Maybe you can come with us always.' To the other he said: 'I know Mikey a long time. He's awright, man.'

The old Indian came back with the cup of tea Michael Adonis had ordered and put it down on the table. Some of the tea had slopped over into the saucer. He looked at the three who had come in, chewing his betel nut. The boy with the scarface looked around at him and said: 'Okay, baas, we going. We want nothing.'

He looked at Michael Adonis again, while the old Indian went away. Then he said: 'We saw some law going into your place. Heard a rooker got chopped or something.'

'And we seen you come out the side lane, too,' the boy with the skull-and-crossbones ring said, with smiling malice.

Michael Adonis stared at them and felt suddenly trapped. On the one hand he would have liked to have proclaimed it to them like a victory over their own petty accomplishments, but on the other hand the mixed feelings of fear and caution gagged him. He did not like the boy with the ring and wanted to tell him that he, Michael Adonis, was a bigger shot now than he was, but he smiled back into the depraved eyes of the boy and said: 'And then? What the hell it got to do with me?'

Foxy reached out and patted the shoulder of his scuffed leather coat and said: 'Mikey's a good boy. He's not like you jubas. He got class. Don't I say Mikey?' Then directly to the two with him: 'Now let's muck off.'

They went over towards the doorway, but before he went out Foxy stopped and turned, smiling again at Michael Adonis.

'You don't have to worry niks, Mikey. We okay. We don't give a eff for the law. You come in with us. We okay.' He waved a hand and then went out through the bead curtains.

Joe had finished his meal now and he looked at Michael Adonis and asked: 'What they talking about, Mikey? That stuff about the law down at your place.'

'I don't know. *Ek weet nie*,' Michael Adonis answered, feeling angry. 'How the hell should I know? I told them, didn't I?'

'Listen, Michael,' Joe said, speaking seriously now, and feeling awkward about it at the same time. 'Listen, maybe you got big troubles. Bigger than I got.' He felt somewhat ashamed of the comparison, but he went on. 'Like I said, we all got troubles. But johns like them don't help you out of them. They in trouble themselves. You'd only add to the whole heap of troubles. I don't know how to tell it, but you run away with them and you got another trouble. Like those rookers. They started a small trouble, maybe, and they run away from it and it was another trouble, so they run away all the time, adding up the troubles. Hell, I don't know.' He felt desperate and a little sad, and did not know quite what to say.

Michael Adonis scowled at him and asked: 'What the blerry hell you know? What troubles you got?'

Joe looked down at the plate which he had wiped clean so that the tiniest morsel of food had not escaped his belly. He said, embarrassed: 'I don't know. I got nothing. No house, no people, no place. Maybe that's troubles. Don't I say?'

'Where's your people, then?' Michael Adonis asked. He tasted his tea, which had gone cold during all the talking.

'Somewhere. I don't know. Hear, we used to live in Prince Lane, mos, a long, long time. Me, my old woman and my father and my sister, Mary, and my small brothers, Isaac and Matty. Then one day my father goes out and he never comes back again. He just went out one morning and we never saw him again.'

'What the hell he do that for?' Michael Adonis asked. 'What for he want to do a thing like that?'

'Don't know. He never mos told us nothing. He just went out that morning and that was the last we saw of him.'

Joe said, shaking his head and frowning, looking at his plate: 'I don't know. Maybe he had troubles, too. He didn't have no job. He was out of a job for a long time and we didn't get things to eat often. Me and my brother Matty used to go out mornings and ask from door to door for pieces of stale bread. Sometimes we got some last-night's cooked food with it from the people. But it was never enough for all of us. My old woman never used to touch the stuff, but shared it out among us lighties. Also the rent of the house wasn't paid and after a while my old woman gets a letter we got to get out. The landlord sends a lot of letters, saying every time we got to clear out, and afterwards some bastards come with a paper and walks right in and stacks all the furniture on the pavement outside and then locks the door and says if we go back we will all be thrown in the jail.'

Joe wasn't happy any more. He looked old and very serious. He said:

'My old woman just sat there by the pile of furniture with Mary and Isaac and Matty and me, and cries. She just sit there and cry. Then after some time she says, Well, we got to go back to the country to stay with my ouma, my grandmother. So she sells the furniture to a secondhand man, and they go away.'

'They?' Michael Adonis said. 'What about you?'

'Me, I ran away when I heard they was going. I just ran away like my old man.' Joe looked at Michael Adonis and said: 'I wasn't going to the outside. To the country. Man, that would be the same like running away, too. Some bastards come with a piece of paper and tell you to get the hell out because you haven't got money for the rent, and a shopkeeper tell you you got to have money else you don't get nothing to eat, and you got to go away somewhere else where it's going to start all over again. No, man,' he shook his head again, 'What's the use. I rather stay around here and starve on one spot or maybe pick up something here and there to get something in my belly. My old man, he ran away. I didn't want to run, too.'

Michael Adonis stared at him for a moment. He felt a little embarrassed now in the presence of this boy. He had never heard Joe say anything as lengthy and as serious as this and he wondered whether the boy had spoken the truth or was a little queer. Then he picked up his neglected cup and drank. The tea was quite cold now and a scum of milk had started to form on the surface.

He said, uncomfortably: 'You like some tea?'

'No thanks, man. It's okay.'

Michael Adonis put his cup down and took out his cigarettes.

He shoved the packet over to Joe and said gruffly: 'Well, have a smoke, then.'

Joe shook his head and smiled gently and somewhat shyly. He said: 'No thanks. I don't mos smoke.' Then he added, serious again: 'You mustn't go with those gangsters, Mikey. You leave those gangsters alone.'

'What's it to you?' Michael Adonis asked, feeling both angry and embarrassed. 'What's it to you?'

'Nothing. Nothing, I reckon. But they mean boys.'

'Ah, hell,' Michael Adonis said and got up. He went over to the counter where the old Indian dozed and got some money out. He paid for his tea, feeling the ragged boy's eyes on him, and did not look back when he went out.

FOURTEEN

Night crouched over the city. The glow of street lamps and electric signs formed a yellow haze, giving it a pale underbelly that did not reach far enough upwards to absorb the stars that spotted its purple hide. Under it the city was a patchwork of greys, whites and reds threaded with thick ropes of black where the darkness held the scattered pattern together. Along the sea front the tall shadows of masts and spars and cranes towered like tangled bones of prehistoric monsters.

Willieboy came up a street that was flanked on one side by the great blank wall of a warehouse, and on the other by a row of single-storied houses fronted by wooden fences. Lights burned in some of the windows and in one of the houses a radio was playing. He went up the street, his hands deep in the pockets of his trousers, pushing the sides of the trousers outwards so that they looked like riding breeches. He was feeling muzzy and his head ached. And felt angry and humiliated by the manhandling he had received at Gipsy's shebeen. He clenched his fists in his pockets and thought, They can't treat a man like that, where can they treat a juba like that? Hell, I'm a shot, too. I'll show those sonsabitches.

He was also aware of his inferiority. All his youthful life he had cherished dreams of becoming a big shot. He had seen others rise to some sort of power in the confined underworld of this district and found himself left behind. He had looked with envy at the flashy desperadoes who quivered across the screen in front of the eightpenny gallery and had dreamed of being transported wherever he wished in great black motorcars and issuing orders for the execution of enemies. And when the picture faded and he emerged from the vast smoke-laden cinema mingling with the noisy crowd he was always aware of his inadequacy, moving unnoticed in the mob. He had affected a slouch, wore gaudy shirts and peg-bottomed trousers, brushed his hair into a flamboyant peak. He had been thinking of piercing one ear and decorating it with a gold ring. But even with these things he continued to remain something less than nondescript, part of the blurred face of the crowd, inconspicuous as a smudge on a grimy wall.

He turned from the street into another equally as gloomy and quiet and up ahead he saw the dark form of somebody approaching along the pavement. It was a man and he was walking with a lurch that sent him from side to side as he came on.

It was with a sense of shock that he came face to face with Willieboy. He pulled up with a hiccough, his mouth dropping open, drooling, and his bloodshot eyes widening with fright. He tried to turn away and run, but his drunken legs would not allow him to, and he lurched awkwardly. Then Willieboy had hold of him by the front of his coat and he wailed in terror.

'Hullo, old man,' Willieboy said. 'Give us five bob, man.'

'No, man, I haven't got, man,' Mister Greene gasped, his voice quavering with fear. He was scared that the boy would pull a knife.

'Come on, pally. Let's have five bob.'

'Please, man. Please.'

Greene tried to pull away, but the boy held onto him, and then suddenly his legs were kicked expertly from under him and he was flat on the pavement with the boy standing over him.

He shouted: 'Please. No, man, No, man.'

Willieboy kicked him viciously in the ribs and he squealed more from fear than pain. Then hands were running through his pockets while he crouched trembling.

'Ah, effit,' Willieboy sneered. 'You bare-arsed bastard. You got nothing.'

'If I had I'd give you, man,' Greene cried. 'Leave me alone, man.'

'I got a good mind to chop you,' Willieboy told him savagely. 'I got a good mind to chop you.'

'Please.'

'Gwan. Muckoff to your wife and kids.'

He kicked Greene again and again, then stood back while the groaning man climbed to his feet. Shock and fear had sobered the haggard man, and he stumbled away, tripping in his haste to get away. Willieboy took a step towards him and he screamed with terror and started to run, gasping painfully. Willieboy watched him running into the darkness and when he had disappeared, turned away down the street.

Willieboy reached the end of the street and turning the corner he saw the police van. It was coming along the rows of shuttered shops and dim tenements, cruising slowly, and the glare of its headlights caught him as he hesitated on the pavement.

FIFTEEN

Michael Adonis was almost at the end of the street when he heard Joe coming after him. One of Joe's shoelaces was loose and it flick-flicked on the asphalt as he ran. He came beside the young man and said, a little breathless: 'Mike. Mikey, listen here . . .'

Walking along the dark street Michael Adonis did not look at him, but thought, Well, what you want now. You reckon you going to be around me for the rest of my blerry life? You spook.

Somewhere up ahead people were singing.

'Mike,' Joe was saying, 'Mike, maybe it isn't my business, you see? Maybe it got nothing to do with me, but you like my brother. I got to mos think about you. Jesus, man, why, you even gave me money for food. There's not a lot of people give me money for food. Awright, maybe now and then. But most of the time I do what I can out on the rocks.'

He was getting out of breath again because Michael Adonis was quickening his pace and the boy, Joe, had to step out to keep up with him. He spoke quickly as if he had very little time in which he had to say what he wanted to say.

'Listen, Mikey,' he said. 'You don't know those boys. They have done bad things. I heard. To girls, also. I heard about Mrs Kannemeyer's daughter. And they use knives, too. They'se a bunch of gangsters, Mike, and they'se going to land up somewhere bad. They was in reformatory, one of them at least. I forget what one. But they'll get you in trouble, Mikey. They break into places and steal, and I heard they stabbed a couple of other johns. Christ, I don't want to see you end up like that, Mike. Hell, a man'd rather starve. They'll murder somebody and get hanged, Mikey. You want to get hanged?'

Michael Adonis suddenly stopped in his stride and looked at Joe.

'What the hell you following me around like a blerry tail for?' he asked angrily. 'What's it got to do with you what I'm going to do?'

'Please, Mike,' Joe said. He looked as if he was going to cry. 'I'm your pal. A man's got a right to look after another man. Jesus, isn't we all people?'

'Ah, go to hell,' Michael Adonis shouted at him. 'Go to hell. Leave me alone.'

He turned his back and went on down the street, leaving Joe staring after him, his face puckering with the beginning of weeping.

Blerry young squashy, Michael Adonis thought as he turned up another street. For what's he got to act like a blerry godfather?

A few blocks further up a street that led back into Hanover was the Club. It was on the ground floor in what had once been a shop. Behind the painted plate-glass windows billiard cues clacked against balls, and a strip of light escaped from under the door. Overhead was an old balcony that fronted a row of shabby rooms.

Michael Adonis tried the door and found it locked. He rattled the knob and waited. It was unlocked and opened a few inches to reveal a part of Foxy's scrofulous face.

'Hoit, Mike,' Foxy said, and opened the door for him to enter. 'Glad you thought it over, pally.'

Inside the two youths were shooting balls across the billiard table. One of them had his coat off, showing the bright metal links of his new armbands. They looked up as Michael Adonis came in. The boy with the skull-and-crossbones ring was leaning on his cue. At the back of the room another man slept on an old disembowelled sofa, breathing harshly through his mouth. The room smelled badly of tobacco smoke and marijuana, which is called dagga here, mingled with the stench of stagnant water from a puddle under a filthy sink in a corner.

Michael Adonis stood under the harsh light of the room, his

hands in the pockets of his leather coat, looking at the two youths. Foxy finished locking the door and came over saying: 'Well, Mikey here's come along, so to hell with Sockies. Don't I say, Mike?'

'I reckon so,' Michael Adonis answered.

'We got a job we going to do later on. Sockies was supposed to hold candle for us while me and these two jubas did the work. He did not turn up, so he can forget it. You coming with us, Mike?'

'Of course, ja, man.'

'Mike's a good juba,' Foxy smiled at the other two, slapping Michael Adonis on the back. 'You'll see. He going to be with us a long time.'

The boy with the ring put his cue aside and felt in the pockets of his trousers, while the other boy went on playing. He got out a packet of cigarette papers and extracted two leaves, returning the rest to the pocket. He arranged the leaves carefully, wetting the end of one and pasting it over an end of the other, thus joining the two into one long strip. He worked with the care of a surgeon performing a delicate operation. Then he formed the strip into a trench, holding it gently between the thumb and third finger of one hand, with the tip of the index finger in the hollow of the trench, keeping it in shape. With his other hand he got out a small cylinder of brown paper and bit off one end, and from it poured some of the dagga evenly along the length of the trench and then put the brown-paper packet away. Next he got out a cigarette and split it with a thumbnail and scattered the tobacco from it onto the dagga, and then mixed the two carefully without spilling any. When he was satisfied he rolled the cigarette paper deftly into a tube, licked one edge with the tip of his tongue and pasted it down, pinched an end shut and stroked the tube caressingly into shape. Then he twisted the other end shut and put it in his mouth and lit it.

He took two long puffs at the dope and let the smoke out through his nostrils in long twin jets. Then he looked at Michael Adonis and said: 'Pull a skuif, pal?'

The other boy had stopped working at the billiard balls, poised over the table about to make a shot, but not finishing it, standing quite still as if a motion picture of him had suddenly been stopped, looking at Michael Adonis.

'Take a pull, pally,' the boy with the skull-and-crossbones ring said again.

'Why not, man?' Michael Adonis said, meeting his look, and reached out. He took a deep puff at the dagga and felt the floor move under him and the walls tilt, then settle back, and there was a light feeling in his head. He took another puff and handed it back to the boy.

'Come on,' Foxy said suddenly. 'That pill's going in a line. I'm next.'

When he had had his share and it had been passed on to the scarfaced boy he said: 'We better talk about this job. We got a car, too, and Toyer is going to drive.' He walked around the billiard table to the back of the room and seized the sleeping man by a shoulder, shaking. 'Come on, you bastard, wake up. Shake it up.'

The man grunted in his sleep, tried to turn over and then opened his eyes when Foxy slapped his face. He said: 'Whatter? Whatter? What goes on, man?'

'Come on. Come on. We got to talk business.'

The man sat up and rubbed his eyes. He asked: 'Sockies turn up?'

'Nay, man. We got another pally. Mikey, here.'

Toyer got to his feet and came towards the front of the room, looking at Michael Adonis. He said: 'Hoit, pally.'

'How's it?' Michael Adonis asked and giggled suddenly. He was feeling happy after the dagga.

The scarfaced boy at the billiard table said quickly: 'What's that?'

They all turned and looked at him. He was staring in front of him, holding the cue underarm, like a rifle, and listening.

'What the hell's the matter with you?' Foxy growled.

'Sounded like somebody shooting,' the scarfaced boy said.

'Shooting. Shit,' Foxy said. 'Who's shooting?'

'Well, it sounded like somebody fired a gun,' the boy told him.

Foxy went to the door, unlocked it and went out. He stood on the pavement and looked up the street for a while. Then he came in again and relocked the door.

He said: 'What you think this is? The bio? Cowboys and crooks?'

'Well, I only said what I heard,' the scarfaced boy replied.

Then they all heard the sound. It sounded like a cannon cracker going off far away, many blocks away in another part of the District. Later it came again, the flat sharp sound of a pistol shot.

SIXTEEN

The driver was glad that they were out of that smelly tenement again and back on patrol. At the same time he was somewhat irritated by the sullen presence of Constable Raalt who nursed gloomy thoughts about his wife. Driving the patrol van, he thought it has to be this one. I have to be put up all night with this one. He's got trouble with his wife, and what have I got to do with his troubles? What has his troubles got to do with this patrol? Let him leave his domestic troubles at home. He is dangerous, too, when he's like this and I don't want to get involved in anything. The way he behaved back there in that place, sneering and putting on in front of those hotnots. That's the way they lose respect. You've got to set an example with these people. Train them like dogs to have respect for you. If you whip them they'll turn on you. You've got to know how to handle these people. Pa knew how to handle these people. I wonder how he's getting on out there on the farm. He's got a lot of these hotnots working out in the orchards and the vineyards and he's never had any trouble with them. Give them some wine and drive them into town Saturday nights and they're all right.

He remembered the long bumpy drive through the wide rich farmlands at dusk in the lorry, swaying and rolling along the dirt roads with the dust boiling up behind in a long dark screen and the farm hands singing and shouting in the back, and the sky growing dark and purple with the first stars beginning to show and the crickets beginning to make their sounds. Only you couldn't hear the crickets then because of the noise of the lorry. Once one of the hands had fallen off the tailgate and they'd had to stop. He'd grazed his head and shoulder on the gravel and was half silly from shock, and the driver's father had cursed him for a donder se blik-sem of a hotnot, and the others had looked on from the back of the lorry, laughing in the growing darkness. They had all called the driver *jong baas*, the young boss, and now and then he had joked with some of them, about their wives and daughters and sweet-hearts, and they always laughed and had never showed any resent-ment. For a while he had thought about sleeping with one of the meide, the girls, but he had never got around to it, and anyway, he thought that it would bring great dishonour upon himself, his family and the volk if ever such a thing was done and discovered. There was a girl in the town who he liked very much, and to whom he now wrote occasional letters. He had not decided whether he was in love with her, for he considered himself a very serious young man and did not wish to fling himself headlong into marriage unless he was absolutely sure. She was beautiful, tall and sun-tanned, with short curly blonde hair and merry eyes and long lovely legs, and he remembered her with some excitement. Still, he did not wish to get himself into the kind of mess Raalt was in, although, the driver thought, this girl was not a woman that would cause a man any misery. He wondered whether he ought to write to her and try to make things permanent, but this thought was interrupted suddenly by Raalt's harsh voice.

'Pull up, man.'

'What?' the driver asked with a start, jamming on the brakes.

'Isn't that not that donder se hotnot, the one with the yellow shirt?'

Constable Raalt was already opening the door and beginning to climb out when the driver looked ahead through the windshield and saw the Coloured boy caught in the glare of the headlights. He saw the brown anonymous face, the short kinky hair and the front of the yellow T-shirt and a jumble of thoughts sprawled through his mind, Yellow shirt; farmhands; hotnots; the lorry; I've got to write to her; that yellow shirt; yellow shirt; a young rooker with a yellow shirt, baas; and Constable Raalt was out of the van shouting:

'Hey, you bogger, stand still there.'

The driver climbed quickly out of the van, slamming the door, and he saw Raalt stepping towards the boy. The Coloured boy stood on the edge of the pavement, his feet widespread and his arms slightly spread, still frozen by the shock of the sudden appearance of the police van. Then the driver saw him duck suddenly as Raalt drew near and his body snapped into action like a released spring and he was going up the street fast.

'Stand still, jong,' Raalt shouted, and started off in pursuit.

The driver dashed after them, running hard. The boy was up ahead, weaving and sprinting, panic speeding him on, and the driver saw with a shock that Constable Raalt was unbuttoning his holster.

He drew up close to Raalt and shouted hoarsely: 'Moenie skiet nie, man. Don't shoot.'

But the pistol came up, its lanyard whipping, and then came the hard flat crack and the tongue of orange-yellow flame.

The boy darted suddenly sideways and was gone down a narrow lane, and when the two policemen reached it they were in time to see him bounding and leaping over piles of refuse and overturned dust-bins. Constable Raalt paused to fire again, but the driver was panting: 'Don't shoot. We'll get him. Keep after him, I'll take the van and circle the block.'

Raalt saw the boy reach the end of the lane and turn up the street beyond and he looked at the driver. What the driver saw in his eyes were what he thought were the fires of hell.

Constable Raalt said, spitting out the words: 'All right man, get the effing van and see if you can catch him.'

The driver dashed back along the street towards the patrol van, saying to himself, Don't let him shoot. I don't want any shooting. He's mad now and there's no knowing what he'll do. But don't let him shoot. Lord, don't let him shoot.

At the end of the lane Constable Raalt paused again, looking up the street. He saw no sign of the boy and started to run again. His wind was good and he was a trained sprinter, and he knew that usually these people did not last very long running. He told himself that the bliksem had probably tired after the first hard effort and had ducked in somewhere to hide. He dropped to a trot, his eyes scanning the rows of buildings on each side of the street.

People, attracted by the sound of the shot, were beginning to come into the street, but Raalt took no notice of them. Voices chattered and laughed, cursed, jeered, but Raalt passed up the street, his eyes restless, watching. He was a hunter now, stalking.

He found another alleyway half-way up the street and he stopped by it. Behind him the procession of onlookers came to a halt. He still had his revolver out and he turned to the crowd for the first time, waving it at them.

'Get back, you donders. You'll get hurt.'

After that he ignored them again and looked up the alleyway. It was a dead-end, running into a blank, plastered wall that was the back of another building. Against it was piled a collection of junk, rotting boxes and packing cases, ruined furniture and decaying mattresses and the usual dust-bins. Constable Raalt drew his flashlight with his left hand and sent the beam around the alley. Walls enclosed it on either side and he stepped forward between them.

He told himself that the boy in the yellow shirt couldn't have got very far down the street in the few moments he had been out of sight, and that he was probably hiding somewhere around. He could have come down an alley such as this one, and this was the first one off the street. Then he heard the sound of movement on the roofs above him, and he flicked off the light, his teeth showing slightly in a tight grin.

Constable Raalt started to mount the pile of rubbish that reached almost to the parapets of the buildings on each side of the alleyway. Behind him the crowd around the entrance of the alley began to scream warnings upwards and he cursed under his breath, looking backwards at them for a moment and climbing quickly. He kicked aside boxes and warped and rotten planking as he ascended, upsetting some of the stacked rubbish. He wondered vaguely where the driver had got to, but he was not concerned with him very much, preferring to hunt alone and undisturbed. He reached the top of the pile and heaved himself upwards to look over a parapet. He saw nothing but the uneven humble of roofs, chimney-pots and drainpipes partly illuminated by the moonlight and street lamps.

Willieboy lay flat on his face, thrusting his body into the hard, unyielding surface of the roof. He felt the rough corrugated iron against his chest through the shirt and coat, and the touch of something cold and metallic against his chin. There was a sour taste in his mouth and his head ached badly. Also, he was out of breath and his chest heaved and jerked from the wild dash down the street and the scramble onto this roof. There was a smell of cat droppings and urine around him. But he noticed none of these things for the cold clutch of fear deep down inside him.

He had dodged the police many times before, but never like this; neither had he been shot at, and he was afraid. He shivered suddenly and his face puckered in the dark, the tears forming in his eyes. He thought, What they want to chase me for? What did I do? I did nothing. I did nothing. What they want to chase me for?

Lying there in the dark he felt the chill of his fear that was colder than the touch of metal or the breeze that had come up over the city.

He thought again, What did I do? I never did nothing. His mind jumped and he saw his mother standing over him, shouting: 'You been naughty again.' He was seven years old and had been selling the evening paper. The sub-agent for whom he hawked the papers had paid him a few pence commission he had earned and he had bought a big parcel of fish and chips instead of taking the money home. He had not eaten since early that morning, and then only a bowl of porridge without milk or sugar and a slice of stale bread, and by evening he was very hungry. He had gone home to the ramshackle room in a tenement with the smell of fish about him and when he could not produce his commission his mother slapped his face and shouted: 'You naughty little bastard.' She slapped him again and again so that his head jerked loosely on his shoulders and his face stung from the blows. He wept through the pain.

His mother beat him at the slightest provocation and he knew that she was wreaking vengeance upon him for the beatings she received from his father. His father came home drunk most nights and beat his mother and him with a heavy leather belt. His mother crouched in a corner of the room and shrieked and whimpered for mercy. When his father was through with her he turned on Willieboy, but sometimes he managed to escape from the room and did not return until late in the night when the father was snoring drunkenly and his mother had cried herself to sleep. His mother, unable to defend herself against her husband, took revenge for her whippings on Willieboy.

Now he lay on the rooftop and heard her again, saying: 'You naughty little bogger.'

He raised a hand and wiped the tears from his eyes. I've got to get away, he told himself, I've got to get away. I don't want to be shot. Please don't let me get shot.

He lay quite still and listened for sounds on the roof. Somewhere below people were shouting and talking, a jumble of words. But he was not concerned about them. He peered ahead around the end of a projection that crossed the roof in front of his face, searching for any sign of the policeman. Once he heard the crunch of a boot on the corrugated iron and fear leapt in him and he tried to force himself into the hard metal under his body. That law's somewhere out there waiting, he thought. What they want to chase me for? I did nothing. You should not have run, he told himself. Soon as you run they come for you. Well I did nothing, I can give myself up. They kick the lights out of you. You think they going to chase you all this way and on top of a roof and then just let you go? Us poor bastards always get kicked around. If it's not the law it's something else. Always there's somebody to kick you around. What kind of blerry business is that? he asked himself with remorse.

Then he heard the policeman's footsteps blundering around on the iron of the roof as he came forward and Willieboy sprang to his feet in fright and dashed for the far end of the row of rooftops.

Constable Raalt had been crouching against an old and disused water tank, waiting for some sign of the boy. He knew for sure that the boy was somewhere on that row of roofs and he waited for him to show himself. Constable Raalt was determined to take his time about this. He had his quarry trapped and he was quite sure that he would conclude the hunt successfully. He crouched there in the dark and smiled with satisfaction.

The water tank was on his left and a few feet to his right was a pigeon loft. He could hear the soft rustling sounds that came from inside it and smell the odour of bird-lime. Below in the street the crowd was moving about growling. For a moment he wondered what had happened to the driver, but he thrust the thought quickly from his mind along with every other thought and concentrated coldly on what he had to do there on the rooftops.

After a while he decided that he would move forward a little. He did not want to turn on the flashlight because he was enjoying this stalk in the dark. He took a long step forward and his face struck a clothes-line, the taut, stretched wire causing him to step back stumbling on the corrugated surface of the roof.

He cursed and ducked under the wire and it was then that he saw the dark form of the Coloured youth spring up from behind a projection ahead of him and start off, bounding across the roofs.

Raalt flung himself forward, firing as he did so. The flash of the pistol made a bright flare of light for a second and the bullet struck a drainpipe and sang off. Then Raalt was running across the roofs, his boots drumming the surface.

A roar went up from the crowd in the street below and a woman screamed shrilly. Raalt pounded on, leaping projections, holding his head low to evade the clothes-lines. He saw the boy poise himself for an instant on the edge of the far wall and drop out of sight.

Willieboy struck the asphalt below and the shock of the awkward drop jarred through his body. A hot stab of pain seared through an ankle and he screamed with pain, then he was stumbling and hobbling crookedly into the middle of the street with the crowd breaking back ahead of him. Then he saw another section of the mob split and the patrol van sweeping down on him.

He turned with fear and despair disfiguring his face, hearing the van screeching to a halt and seeing Constable Raalt drop expertly from the roof he had left. He stared bewilderedly about him. Then with the policemen moving on him from the front and back he crouched like a fear-crazed animal at bay and shouted hysterically at the one with the gun:

'You . . . boer. You . . . boer.'

He cursed Constable Raalt, unloading the obscenities like one dumping manure and then reached frantically for the pocket where he carried the sharpened kitchen-knife.

Before his hand reached the pocket and before he could discover that the knife was not there Constable Raalt fired again.

The bullet slapped into the boy, jerking him upright, and he spun, his arms flung wide, turning on his toes like a ballet dancer.

SEVENTEEN

The crowd roared again, the sound breaking against the surrounding houses. They wavered for a while and then surged forward, then rolled back, muttering before the cold dark muzzle of the pistol. The muttering remained, the threatening sound of a storm-tossed ocean breaking against a rocky shoreline.

'Shot him in cold blood, the bastards.'

'They just know to shoot.'

'Is he dead?'

'How the hell do I know.'

'Move over, I want to see.'

'Shot him down in cold blood.'

'Awright, they'll get it, one day. You'll see.'

'Who is it, anyway?'

'Don't know. Some rooker they was chasing.'

'Must have been one of those skollies. Always interfering with people. They all end up like that. Did he have a knife?'

'Shot the poor bastard in cold blood.'

'That's all they know. Shooting us people.'

'Move over, man. I also want to see mos.'

'Stop shoving. The bastards.'

The mutter of dark water eroding the granite cliffs, sucking at the sand-filled cracks and dissolving the banks of clay.

The driver had a shocked look on his face and he said, his voice cracking: 'What did you want to shoot for? We had him. I could have got him from behind.'

Constable Raalt told him. 'What's the matter with you, Andries? Aren't you a policeman?' His eyes were hard and grey, like two rough pebbles in the dark, and his mouth was bitter.

The driver looked down at the boy. He lay groaning, holding himself where he had been shot, and a pool of blood was forming under him, spreading on the asphalt.

'Jesus, man,' the driver said. 'We'd better call an ambulance.'

'Ambulance,' Constable Raalt scoffed. 'Hell, we'll take the

bliksem down to the station. They'll patch him up. He's not hurt so terribly.'

'I think we'd better call an ambulance,' the driver insisted nervously. He looked as if he was about to cry.

Then Willieboy suddenly screamed aloud. 'Oh mamma, oh, mamma,' he screamed. 'It hurts. Oh, my mamma, my mamma.'

The crowd surged forward again, growling, and then fell back under the hard, threatening muzzle of Constable Raalt's pistol. Somebody threw a tin can and it curved over the milling heads and struck the fender of the police van.

'You bastards,' Raalt shouted, waving the revolver. 'You bastards, you want to get shot, too?'

The driver was worried, and he said: 'Come on, man, let's go. Let's go.'

He looked down at the boy who had been shot. The front of the yellow shirt was dark with blood and there was some blood on the edge and lapels of his coat. He had fainted and in the light of the headlamps his face bore a stark, terrible look, the skin coarse and drawn tight so that the bone structure of the adolescent, undeveloped face showed gauntly, covered with a film of sweat.

The driver said: 'Christ, man, we'd better hurry up. Get him out of here. We ought to call an ambulance, I say.'

'Muck the ambulance,' Constable Raalt snapped. 'Load him in the back of the van and take him down to the station. They'll fix him up there, the bloody hotnot.'

'We'd better go,' the driver repeated impatiently. 'I don't like this crowd.'

'This crowd. A lot of bloody baboons. All right, man, let's get this bogger into the back. You take him by the feet.'

The driver stooped quickly and took the boy by his ankles. He was in a hurry to get away from there, and felt nervous and anxious. Raalt bent over the boy's head and gripped the collar of his coat, hauling him roughly into a sitting position. His other hand still held the pistol, and his eyes watched the murmuring crowd. The driver raised the boy and they carried him, his limp body sagging in the middle like a half-empty sack, to the back of the van. Around them the crowd rolled forward again and the driver prayed that there wouldn't be any more shooting. He told himself that Raalt was crazy to have shot the youth and that there would probably be a hell of a lot of trouble over this.

They got the double doors of the van open and bundled the unconscious boy into the back. In his hurry to get away the driver pushed and thrust him quickly, so that he rolled and flopped on the bed of the van, groaning. They slammed the doors and came around to the driving cabin, Raalt still holding the gun, watching the sullen crowd.

The driver was in the cabin first, fumbling with the ignition in his hurry and grinding the gears. Beside him Constable Raalt holstered his pistol and the van moved forward into the crowd. The driver was still scared and nervous and he caused the van to bounce and jerk, scattering the people around it and raising an uproar. Fists thumped on the metal bodywork and a shower of brickbats rained suddenly down on it, but the driver got the vehicle under control and ploughed slowly through the mob.

EIGHTEEN

'You was naughty again,' his mother shouted and slapped his face so that pain leapt through him. He stood against the door jamb of the ugly room, rubbing one stubby-toed bare foot against the instep of the other and wept, wiping his running nose on the ragged, filthy sleeve of his khaki shirt.

The inside of the van was dark and there was no sound but the purr of the motor. There was something cold and metallic against his cheek, which conjured up a vague recollection of rooftops, but he did not know what it was, nor did he attempt to find out. He did not move his head and did not try to wipe his running nose. The effort was too much for him, and when he moved his head he vomited and his head spun so that he would go into a coma. So he rode with the pain that lapped at him. It was a dull formless pain that caressed him, trembling through his body with the throbbing of the van's engine. There was another pain in his ankle but it had the feeling of being apart from the rest of his body.

He wanted to get up and go home, but he decided there was no point in going home because his father would only beat him again. He'd go down to the Daffodil Club and play some billiards, or get a drink. He could do with a drink. His head ached and he had a very bad hangover, and there was this pain rolling backwards and forwards, up and down inside him, like a loose, heavy iron bearing in a cylinder.

Through the dull pain the coldness against his cheek was irritating and he decided to turn his head in order to discover what caused it. It was caused by one of the metal strips that were fixed on the floor of the van, but before he could realize that, he choked and bile filled his mouth, welling up and bursting from the corner of his lips. He tried to sit up, but could not, and the bile receded into his throat so that he retched and the pain lanced him as his body twitched and he screamed and fainted.

The patrol van was in Hanover Street again, passing between the rows of locked shops with their lighted glass box-signs and price-cards and the peeling placards, and above them the rows of shabby rooms behind painted-over glass doors and splintering and reinforced balconies; past the dark public houses and black caverns of tenement hallways, the cafes with dim lights behind the beaded curtains and soda-fountain parlours with late customers sipping bottled drinks, leaning against the marble-topped counters and the display stands; past the street corners where the knots of youths lounged, smoking and laughing, the laughter breaking off to be replaced by silent stares in the dark as the police cruised by; past the neon sign that said Coca-Cola, Coca-Cola, Coca-Cola over and over throughout the night.

Constable Raalt felt in his tunic pocket for his cigarettes and found that he had none. He said: 'Pull up at the Portuguese, will you? I want to get some smokes.'

'Jesus, man,' the driver said. 'We haven't got time to get cigarettes. We've got to get this jong to the station.'

'Ach, there's lots of time, man. That bastard isn't going to die yet. These hotnots are tough. Stop at the damn cafe, man.'

The driver shook his head. He was worried and nervous and a little frightened, but he knew that it was no use arguing with Raalt. He said: 'Well, it's your responsibility then,' thereby purging himself of all blame for whatever had happened or might happen afterwards. Constable Raalt looked sideways at him, and smiled, curling his lips from his teeth.

The driver shook his head again and did not look at Raalt, but he slowed down and brought the van to a stop.

'Don't be long, man,' he said keeping his eyes away from Constable Raalt's face. He heard Raalt climbing out, slamming the door of the cabin and cross the pavement into the restaurant.

In the back of the van Willieboy had come to with the small jolt the stopping had made. He awoke with the faint smell of petrol and carbon-monoxide in his nostrils. It made him retch again and he shook until the retching turned to weeping and he cried, the sobs wrenching at him, jerking the pain through his abdomen. He reached down to where the pain was worst and felt the wet stickiness of his clothes and then the bleeding mouth of the wound where the bullet had torn through him, smashing into his insides. Then he seemed to realize for the first time what had happened to him.

'Help! Oh, God, help me! Oh, mamma, oh, mamma. Oh, Lord Jesus, save me. Save me. I'm dying! I'm dying! Save me. Save me. Oh, Christ, help me. Help me. Help me. Please. Help me. God. Jesus. Mother. Help me! Help me!'

His screams crashed against the sides of the van, confined within the metal walls. His father's leather belt whistled and snapped through the air, its sharp edge ripping at his legs and buttocks, the pain jumping through him.

Constable Raalt had entered the cafe. The place was quiet and there were only a few people scattered in the booths and at the long table down the middle of the room. Heads and eyes glanced at him before returning to the chipped cups, the bottles of icy soft drinks and the stale doughnuts. A taxi-driver read the evening paper and did not look up from it when Raalt came in. The fat proprietor behind the counter wiped its marble top and nodded at the constable.

'Hullo,' Raalt said, grinning and pushing his cap back on his head. 'Give us a packet of twenties, please.'

The fat man dropped the package of cigarettes on the counter and asked: 'How's things, meneer?'

'So so,' Constable Raalt told him. 'Always blerry trouble with the skollies up here.'

He broke open the packet and worked a cigarette out of it, stuck it in his mouth and searched for his matches. The Portuguese pushed a box over towards him and he lit the cigarette, puffing.

'Always got trouble with those skollies,' the proprietor said. 'Me, I've got me a nice fish-club under this counter. They don't mess with me. Just the other night a bogger came in here . . .' He began to relate the incident which had taken place.

While they were talking the door opened again and the driver came in. He was looking frightened and his young face had a shocked expression on it.

He said to Raalt: 'We must go, man. That jong . . .'

'What's the hurry?' the cafe proprietor asked, leaning his thick arms on the counter.

Constable Raalt said: 'We've got one of those blerry skollies in the wagon.' To the driver he said: 'What are you looking so troubled about, man?'

'Look, Raalt,' the driver said. 'That jong . . . we'd better get him to the station quickly, man.'

'Hell,' Raalt said maliciously.

The proprietor asked amiably: 'Would you gents like a Coke?'

Willieboy allowed himself to ride with the pain. It was not so bad any more and had taken a dull, numbing character. He felt cold, however, and wished that his mother would spare another blanket to warm him. The rain beat against the window of the tenement room and he shivered under the thin scrap of blanket on the floor. On the bed his father and mother slept together in a bulky jumble. Once his mother woke up and turning her head shouted at him to stop complaining. He said: 'I'm cold, ma,' but received no further reply.

Delirium was an anaesthetic and he no longer felt pain. But his fingers and hands seemed to have thickened and begun to lose all sense of feeling, so that even when he knew that he moved them over his body they did not seem to touch anything. They were like thick, swollen, lifeless things. Also he had difficulty in seeing the darkness inside the van, and there was a high-pitched ringing sound running through his brain.

'They's always kicking a poor bastard around,' he said, and was surprised at the loudness and clarity of his voice. He tried to look through the darkness but the power of sight had gone from his eyes. They remained open although he could no longer see. Then his mouth was suddenly full of bile and blood and he tasted the sourness and the salt for an infinitesimal instant before he was dead.

NINETEEN

Now, after midnight, it was cooler. A breeze had sprung up out of the south-east and stirred the hot air, but the stars remained bright, flickering and shimmering so that the sky was alive with them. In the gutters of the District ragged ends of paper stirred and whispered in the breeze and in the windows of the sweaty tenements, greasy curtains undulated. On the sagging bedsteads and the cramped staircases the sleeping moved and turned in their slumber, sensing the coolness in the air. If the breeze held on and strengthened it would develop into the old summer South-easter by the morning.

At the Club the painted glass doors rattled gently and Foxy commented idly: 'I reckon she's going to blow tomorrow.'

'We'd better blow ourselves,' the youth with the skull-and-cross-bones ring said. 'We going to stand here all blerry night?'

'Awright. Awright,' Foxy said. 'Let's go then.' He looked at Toyer and asked: 'You sure the car's okay?'

'It's okay, man,' Toyer replied. He was feeling sleepy and yawned loudly. 'Parked around the block.'

'Well, we better blow.' Foxy smiled at Michael Adonis and winked.

'You ready, pally?'

'Naturally. Why not? What about these scared boggers?'

'Who's scared?' the boy with the scarred face asked. Then added sullenly: 'Your mother, man.'

'And yours too, pally,' Michael Adonis said, smiling, and led the way to the door.

They all went out and Foxy turned off the lights and locked the door. He stood on the pavement with the rest of them and looked up at the sky. 'Ja,' he announced. 'It's going to blow.'

From a crack under the skirting-board in a dark room a cockroach emerged cautiously, feeling through the gloom with its antennae, the fine hairlike wands waving this way and that, searching for an obstruction. Finding none, the cockroach moved forward on its jointed, angled legs, crossing the floor, stepping over the tiny hedges caused by the splintered sides of the floorboards. It encountered some stickiness and it tasted the mixture of spilled liquor and vomit on the floor of the room of the slain old man. The old man's body had been removed earlier and the room locked by the police, and now the cockroach was alone in it, with the smell of decay and death. The cockroach paused over the stickiness and a creaking of boards somewhere startled it, sending it scuttling off with tiny scraping sounds across the floor. After a while the room was silent again and it returned and commenced to gorge itself.

In a downstairs room John Abrahams lay with his face towards the wall. He could not sleep and he stared at the dim blankness near his eyes. He had not undressed and he could smell the sweatiness of his clothes and the staleness of the ruin that was his body. He thought dully, What's it help you, turning on your own people? What's it help you? He kept on thinking the same thought over and over again, so that after a while he did not have to put any more effort into thinking because the thought just went on and on its own, What's it help you? What's it help you? What's it help you?

Somewhere the young man, Joe, made his way towards the sea, walking alone through the starlit darkness. In the morning he would be close to the smell of the ocean and wade through the chill, comforting water, bending close to the purling green surface and see the dark undulating fronds of seaweed, writhing and swaying in the shallows, like beckoning hands. And in the rock pools he would examine the mysterious life of the sea things, the transparent beauty of starfish and anemone, and hear the relentless, consistent pounding of the creaming waves against the granite citadels of rock.

Franky Lorenzo slept on his back and snored peacefully. Beside him the woman, Grace, lay awake in the dark, restlessly waiting for the dawn and feeling the knot of life within her.

Tattoo Marks and Nails

The heat in the cell was solid. It was usually hot in the cells, what with over one hundred prisoners packed in, lying on the concrete floor like sardines in a can or tangled like macaroni. But it was the middle of summer, and a week-end when prisoners are locked up early in the day until the following morning, there being only a skeleton staff of guards on duty; it was doubly, perhaps trebly hotter than usual.

The heat was solid. As Ahmed the Turk remarked, you could reach out before your face, grab a handful of heat, fling it at the wall, and it would stick.

The barred windows of the caserne were high up the walls, against the ceiling, and covered by thick wire mesh, its tiny holes themselves clogged and plugged with generations of grime.

We were all awaiting trial. The fact that all such prisoners were deprived of their clothes every time they were locked up in the cells did not make much difference. Naked bodies, or half-naked, only allowed the stench of sweat from close-packed bodies to circulate more freely.

'I know of only one place hotter than this,' said Ahmed the Turk, alleged housebreaker, assaulter and stabber. He smiled, flashing his teeth the colour of ripe corn in his dark handsome face. 'And I don't mean Hell,' he added.

Around us were packed a human salad of accused petty-thieves, gangsters, murderers, rapists, burglars, thugs, drunks, brawlers, dope-peddlars: most of them by no means strangers to the cells, many of them still young, others already depraved, and several old and abandoned, sucking at the disintegrating, bitter cigarette-end of life.

Now and then pandemonium would reign: different men bawling different songs, others howling or talking at the top of their voices, just for the sake of creating an uproar, others quarrelling violently and often fighting. Here and there parties crouched over games of tattered packs of hand-made or smuggled cards, draughts played with scraps of paper or chips of coal as counters on boards scraped on the floor.

Pandemonium would abdicate for a while when the guard reached the cell door on his rounds around the section and shouted through the peephole in the iron-bound door.

I wiped sweat from my face with a forearm and said: 'You were saying something about a place hotter than this.'

'Ja,' replied Ahmed the Turk. 'Wallahi. Truly.'

'And where would that be?' I asked. 'On top of a primus stove?'

'No man,' Ahmed replied. 'In the Italian prisoner-of-war camp by Wadi Huseni in Libya. I was mos there during the War.'

At the other end of the caserne, The Creature, so named after some fantastic and impossible monster of the films, and his gang were persecuting some poor wretch who had arrived that morning. The man, not as smart as others, not able to catch the wire, know the ropes, had been locked up with not even an undershirt on his body. He cringed, stark naked, before The Creature and his henchmen.

The gang-leader, and incidentally cell-head by virtue of his brutality and the backing of equally vicious hangers-on, was pointing at the poor joker's bare chest on which something colourfully gaudy had been tattooed, and snarling above the other noises in the cell: 'Listen, you jubas, there's only one tattoo like that in the whole blerry land, I bet you . . .'

'What's that basket up to?' I asked.

Ahmed the Turk stuck a crippled cigarette-end between his lips and struck a split match expertly on the wall. 'Going to hold a court, I reckon,' he said, blowing smoke. 'Never liked these —— prison courts.'

A common occurrence in prisons was the 'trial', by the most brutalized inmates, of some unfortunate who might have raised their ire by bootlicking a guard, or rightly or wrongly accused of giving evidence against, squealing on, his fellow prisoners, or having annoyed them in some other way. Mock courts, much more dangerous than real ones, were held in the cells and 'sentence' meted out.

There had been the 'case' of a prisoner who had given offence to a cell-boss and his gang. It had been said that he had complained of them to a guard, an unforgivable offence. The gangsters 'tried' him, found him guilty and sentenced him to . . . he wasn't told. That, as some sadistic refinement, they kept secret among themselves.

The terrified man died a hundred times over before, finally, unable to hold back weariness, he was forced to lie down to sleep. As he lay shivering in some unknown nightmare, a blanket was pressed over his head and face, and a half-dozen knives driven through the one in which he slept.

The next morning the guards found a dead man wrapped in a bloody blanket. No trace of blood on any of the rest of the packed humanity in the cell. There was no sign of a knife. Nobody had a knife, despite searches. The prison inquiry revealed nothing.

'Dammit,' I said, taking what was left of the butt from Ahmed. 'Hell, that rooker just come in. They got nothing on him.'

'Maybe he done something to them outside,' the Turk reckoned. He added, 'There was a court at Wadi Huseni, too.

'Forget them,' he advised, but he was listening to what The Creature was yelling at his gang and the grovelling victim. Then he smiled at me again.

'I was telling you about the P.O.W. camp by Wadi Huseni. Pally, there it was hot. Yellow sand and yellow sky. Man, just sand and sky and some thorn bushes, maybe. And the sun.

'I was in the Coloured Corps, mos, during the War. Lorry driver. Well, some blerry Eyeties supporting the Germans captured us at the time of the Rommel business. So they take us to this camp. A square of barb-wire fence with guards walking round and round it all the time. It was full of our men, Aussies, English and others. And the sun, chommy. Burning, boiling, baking, frying, cooking, roasting.

'The Eyeties lived in tents near the prisoners' camp. We, we had no shelter, nothing man. They fixed up a shelter with sailcloth for the sick and wounded. The rest had to do what they could. Understand?'

Ahmed the Turk grinned. 'You call this hot, chommy? Pally, we used to cut slices off the heat, put them on our biscuits and make toast.'

I laughed, and wiped some more moisture from my nose. Ahmed the Turk smiled again and scratched himself under his once-gaudy, now grimy and sweat-stained shirt which he had managed to hang onto since he'd come in. He never got out of that shirt.

The Creature was yelling, '. . . Don't lie, you basket . . . We know . . . Hear me. I said somebody chopped my brother, Nails, in the back with a knife . . . In the back, don't I say? . . . Over some blerry goose. Nails' goose, right? . . . The whore . . .'

'The Creature's saying up big likely,' Ahmed the Turk said. 'His brother, Nails. Just a big mouth like The Creature is, he was. But he had a nice girl, anyway.'

'. . . Couldn't say his name before he died . . . But that he had a dragon picked out on his chest, pally . . . a dragon, right? . . . Maybe like the one *you* got.'

'It wasn't me,' the naked prisoner babbled.

'Did you know his brother, Nails?' I asked.

'Yes, man,' Ahmed the Turk replied. 'Seen him around. Nails, tattoos, courts.' He laughed. 'Listen, chommy, it reminds me of that court in Wadi Huseni that time.

'Like I was saying, man, it was hot, hot, hot. Water reshun, one tin cup a day. Hot. Hot. Hot.

'After some time, the water supply runs down and the Eyeties are only handing out half-a-cuppy a day. Man, half-a-cuppy. Food they could keep. Biscuits and sardines. But water, man. Water.'

Ahmed the Turk sighed and flicked a rivulet from his brow. The water bucket in the cell itself had just been emptied of the last mouthful and the crowd around it was growling and snapping like mongrels.

The Creature was laughing. It was he who had collared the last of the water, and he was laughing merrily at the others. Then he turned back to his 'prisoner'.

'. . . Right in the back, hey? . . . Nails said we'd know you by that dragon on your chest . . . Well, we's got you now, pally . . .' He laughed again, the sound coming from his throat like the screeching of a hundred rusty hinges.

'I don't know nothing from it,' the man whimpered. 'True as God, ou pal.'

The Creature went on laughing.

'I was telling about the water shortage,' Ahmed resumed. 'Yes, man. Half-a-cuppy a day in the middle of that seven kinds of Hell.'

I said, 'You reckoned the tattoo stuff reminded you of something.'

'I'm coming to that, man,' he said. 'Listen. After a while it got so everybody was getting pretty desperate for water, hey.

'Then some joker comes up with a scheme. He got a pack of cards, old, dirty, cracked, but still a full deck. 'Let's play for the water reshun,' this joker say. 'Half-a-cup of water is the limit, and winner takes the lot. Anybody want to play?'

Ahmed the Turk smiled. 'There was helluva lot of jubas in that camp wasn't going to take any chances with their water in a card game. Understand? No, pally. They stuck to what they had. But there was some other desperate johns willing to take a chance.

'Further, later on there's quite a clump in the game when the Eyeties have handed out the water. Well, somebody's got to win a card game, don't I say? And one of the boys has a merry old time with nearly two pints of water that he wins.

'Next day the joker with the deck is ready for a game again, quick as the water was handed out. Another rooker wins this time.

'Well, pally, for a couple of days different johns are winning water, and a lot of birds lose their rations. But they are still willing to play.

'Then all of sudden, the luck of the joker who owns the deck changes, and he starts to win the whole pot every day, day after day. Oh, he has a time awright. And with all the losers looking on, likely.

'Dammit, he had water so he could use some of it just to pour over his head like a shower bath, mos. And never parted with a drop of water to the other burgs. There are jokers going crazy for an extra drop in that camp. But our friend just has himself a grand time winning water from a lot of squashies.

'Until the other johns start to think about it.'

Ahmed the Turk laughed again and scratched under his shirt. He went on: 'Maybe they start reckoning it's funny for this joker to keep on winning all the time. Further, these johns are getting more and more desperate, having no water.

'So, it happens, after the joker had won another game and is pouring his winnings into a big tin he'd got for the purpose, one of the gang, a big Aussie, say: 'Look, cobber. Let's take a look at the deck, hey?'

'The joker looks up at the Aussie, while he is pouring cups of water into his tin, and reckons: "What deck, hey? What about the deck? What for you want to see the deck? The deck's okay, man."

' "Let's see the deck, cobber," the Aussie says. A big boy, like most of those Aussies are. And everybody else is quiet now, looking at the joker, some of them grinning through their beards and their dusty and broken lips.

'Well, "The hell with you," the joker reckons and starts to get up. The next thing, the Aussie lets go with a fist as big and hard as a brick.'

Ahmed the Turk grinned, showing his teeth, and rubbed his jaw, brushing sweat from it and wiping the moist hand on the front of his shirt. At the other end of the caserne, The Creature and his gang were still worrying the naked man, like a pack of dogs with a rat.

'What about the tattoo marks?' I asked. I was beginning to eye him with suspicion now.

'I'm coming to that, man,' he replied, scowling across to where

The Creature and his inquisition were in session. 'That pig . . . Anyway, pally, so this Aussie lets blow with his fist.

'Further, when this joker wakes up, he is flat on his back on the sand with his shirt off, and what's more, he is being held down like that by some of the boys. And looking up, he can see this big Aussie standing over him, smiling and fanning out the deck of cards in his big hands. The joker can't make a move with the men holding him down.

'Then further, the Aussie says: "Cobber, playing with marked decks, hey? Cheating your pals out of water, hey? Well, cobber, we sort of held a court martial right here, in your—er—absence. Well, cobber, the court has found you guilty, and we're about to carry out the sentence, cobber." And the Aussie laughs, likely, and everybody else laughs. Except the card joker, naturally. So they carry out the sentence.'

'What was it?' I asked.

Ahmed the Turk scowled. 'Why, this Aussie has got a kind of a knife made from a six-inch flattened nail. And he uses this to well—not actually to do some tattooing on the joker's chest—but really some carving.

'Ja, man. They write it on his chest with that long nail, deep into the flesh so it would never go away, while he's struggling and screaming: PRIVATE SO-AND-SO, A CHEAT AND A COWARD. And the joker got to carry those words in scars around with him long as he lives.'

I gazed at Ahmed the Turk. Then, 'Jesus,' I said. 'What happened to the joker afterwards?'

Ahmed shrugged. 'He escaped. He couldn't stand it, living among those other P.O.W.'s after that, I reckon. Maybe the basket was collecting that water to get away across the desert, in any case.

'Anyway, soon afterwards, he's gone. Got through the wire somehow, and gone he is.' Ahmed the Turk paused. 'That's why I said this court of The Creature, and Nails, and tattooing reminded me also of Wadi Huseni.'

'Ahmed,' I asked him. 'What was the joker's name?'

'I forget now.'

He was gazing across the muttering, heaving, writhing tangle of perspiring prisoners to where the gang was holding their 'court.'

'Turk,' I said again to him, quietly. 'I never did, and nobody here ever did see you with your shirt off, have they?' I was looking at his sweat-stained shirt.

He looked back at me and grinned. 'Hell, man. Why should I take it off? Might get pinched. Besides, it isn't as hot here as it was in that Wadi Huseni camp, mos.' He looked again across at the court. 'Never did like these prison trials,' he muttered. Then shouted: 'Creature, you pig! Why don't you leave the poor basket alone? Can't you see he's . . . scared?'

The Creature looked across at us, his mob flanking him, the poor naked john grovelling and crying. Then he laughed and turning away from his victim, began picking a path among the packed prisoners, towards where we squatted. The gang trailed after him, ignoring the naked man. He couldn't get away, could he? The noise in the cell had dropped to an apprehensive mutter.

The Creature made his way across, kicking bodies and legs out of his path, swearing at the impeding jumble of humanity.

He was half naked, wearing a pair of filthy pajama pants, and over it a pair of khaki shorts confiscated from another unfortunate. A ludicrous sight, yet dangerous as a rabid dog. His face was disfigured and reminded one of a tangled knot of rope, with some of the crevices filled in, topped by a blue, badly shaven skull. He came up, sneering with rotten teeth.

Then he stopped, looking at Ahmed the Turk, and laughed.

He said, 'Turk, I been sizing you up a long time, mos, Turk. Ou Turk, you reckon mos you a hardcase.'

Ahmed the Turk laughed at him. The Creature breathed hard into his big chest, and laughed again in return, so that the rope-knot face squirmed and quivered like some hideous jelly.

'Turk,' he went on. 'Turk, somebody chopped my brother, Nails, in the back. Don't I say? Only thing poor ou Nails knew about the juba he had something picked out, tattooed on his chest, man. A dragon, poor ou Nails said.

'Well, Turk, me I been looking for this pig. Don't I say? When I get him, me and my men going to hold court, inside or outside, 'cording to where we get him.'

Ahmed the Turk grinned. 'What the hell it's got to do with me?' There was a lot of sweat on his face, and he wiped it away, leaving a dirty smear.

The Creature eyed him. 'Turk, you been saying up a lot since you come in here . . . Okay, youse a big-shot, mos . . . But I been hearing things around, ou Turk. I been hearing things like you was messing around ou Nails' goose, also. Don't I say? Okay. Awright. Maybe it's just talk, hey?'

He laughed again, and then went on. 'Okay, Turk, youse a big-shot, mos, outside.' Then he repeated more or less, my own recent request of Ahmed the Turk. 'Come to think about it, Turk. Nobody seen you here with that shirt off, hey? Why don't you take off your shirt, Turk? It's mos hot here, man. Don't I say? Or maybe you heard outside there was word around I was looking for a juba with stuff tattooed on his chest. A dragon, maybe, Turk? Why don't we see you with that shirt off, Turk?'

Ahmed the Turk licked moisture from his lips. He said, 'The hell with you.'

'Turk,' The Creature said. 'Turk, my boys can hold you while we pull off the shirt. Just as you like, ou Turk.'

The gang edged nearer, surrounding us. Ahmed the Turk

looked at The Creature and then looked at me. His face was moist.

Then he laughed, and pulled himself up from his cramped position.

'Awright, all you baskets,' he sneered, and unbuttoned his shirt.

At the Portagee's

'You can have the one in the green,' Banjo said.

'She's got pimples.'

'But she's got mos knobs, too. Don't I say?'

'Well, all right, then.'

'You better talk to them when we go over,' Banjo reckoned. 'You talk to them.'

'What's the matter with you?' I asked. 'Haven't you picked up a goose yet?'

'You talk to them, man.'

We were sitting at a table in this cafe. Banjo had just finished a plate of steak and chips, and I had had an egg roll. Now we were finishing the coffee. There were other people in the cafe, too, and the two girls sat opposite each other at a table in one of the booths down the side of the room. There were empty Coca Cola bottles on the table between them, and one of the girls was looking at herself in a small mirror. The one in green.

There was a smell of cooking in the room, you know, oil and

fried bacon and boiled vegetables and coffee. The ceiling was hung with streamers of fly-paper.

'What are you going to say to them?' Banjo asked.

'I don't know. What must I say?'

'Ask them if they'd like a cold drink,' Banjo reckoned.

'They just had coke,' I told him, looking across at the girls.

'You think we'll strike a luck?'

'I don't know! You think every goose is going to give you that?'

'Don't you want?' he grinned.

While I was thinking of how to go about it a man came into the cafe. He was thin and dirty and wore an old navy-blue suit that was shiny with wear and grease. His face was covered with a two-day beard. He hesitated for a moment, just inside the doorway, and then came over to us. Banjo was watching the girls.

When the man came up he was just like this: 'Say, old pal, spare a sixpence for a bite, man.' He looked tired and his eyes were bloodshot, the eyelids rimmed with red. The cuffs of his jacket were torn and the threads dangled over his wrists.

'Who you bumming from?' Banjo asked, looking up. 'From who do you bum?'

'Leave him alone,' I said. 'What's a sixpence?' I felt in my pockets and found a sixpence among my change and handed it to the man.

He said, 'Thanks, old pally,' not looking at Banjo. 'Gawd bless you, old pal.' He nodded at me and then went to another table and sat down.

'You rich,' Banjo reckoned to me. 'Lord blerry Muck.'

'Ach, never mind, man.'

We looked at the girls again. One of them looked our way and I smiled at her. She looked away and said something to her friend. The other girl looked across at us.

'There's our chance,' Banjo muttered, trying to look as if he wasn't interested.

Some people brushed past our table on their way out of the cafe. Outside the sun was going down. The man in the navy-blue suit sat stiffly at his table waiting to be served.

'Come on,' Banjo pleaded. 'Let's go over, man.'

'Okay,' I said. 'Okay.'

I got up and he did the same and we went over to the girls. Banjo kept behind me, and I could feel my heart beating with embarrassment. The girls didn't look at us.

'Hullo,' I said. 'Can we sit here?'

They still kept looking away, but smiled faintly. The one in the green was watching the other, and this one said, 'Well, it's not our cafe, and there's no reserved seats.'

'Thanks, miss.'

I winked at Banjo and slipped in beside the girl in the green dress and he sat down next to her friend.

'You like a cold drink?' Banjo asked.

They looked at each other again and the girl next to Banjo said, 'well, we just had some cokes.'

'You can have another one mos,' I said.

'Do you want?' she asked the one in green.

'Awright.'

'You get them,' I told Banjo.

'Okay.'

While Banjo was getting the drinks over at the counter I told the girls our names. The one in the green was called Hilda, and her friend was Dolores.

'That's a nice name,' I said to the one called Dolores. 'Spanish mos.'

When Banjo came back with the bottles of mineral water I told him, 'This is Hilda and Dolores.'

'That's fine,' he reckoned and smiled at them. 'You can call me Banjo.'

'His name is Edward Isaacs,' I told them. 'But we just call him Banjo.'

'Does he play the banjo?' Hilda asked.

'I never heard him yet,' I replied, laughing at them. 'He can play the fool all right.'

We sipped the drinks through the straws. While we were talking I heard somebody saying, 'You can't get sixpence food here, you bladdy fool,' and it was the fat Portagee who owned the cafe talking to the tired-looking man in the navy-blue suit. The Portagee was standing by his table and looking across. He was very fat and wore a greasy apron around his belly, and his face was red and sweaty. The waiter who worked there stood nearby.

The man in the tattered navy-blue suit looked at the Portagee and said clearly, 'I only wanted sixpence fish.'

'No sixpence fish,' the Portagee said. 'You better get out.'

He reached out to take the man by the shoulder, but the man moved back on his chair and said, 'Don't touch me. I have done nothing wrong.'

'Get out, you loafer.'

'All right, man,' the man said and got up. 'There's no need to get angry. I'll go.' He spoke with contempt, looking at the Portagee, and then he turned about and walked out of the cafe, holding himself very straight. Some people in the place laughed.

'There goes your sixpence,' Banjo said.

'That poor man,' Hilda said. 'That Greek could have but given him a sixpence fish.'

Banjo began to narrate: 'I heard of a juba who went to a posh cafe in town but he never bought nothing. He was one of those cheap johns, see? He took his own sandwiches with him, and when the waiter come round he ask for a glass of water. Then when the waiter come back with the water, this juba look around and say, "And why ain't the band playing?" '

They didn't smile or say anything and Banjo grinned at me. Then he asked, 'You want to hear the juke-box?'

'Yes,' Dolores said. 'Play *Beyond the Reef*. They got the record in the machine.'

'Okay.'

Banjo got up again and went over to the big juke-box and shoved a sixpence into the slot. The record dropped and the arm swung onto it, and we were listening to Bing.

'He sings real awake,' Hilda said, giggling a little.

'I like Tony Martin,' Banjo reckoned.

We didn't say anything for a while, listening to the voice from the juke box . . . *where the sea is dark and cold* . . . shoving past the other sounds in the cafe. Banjo was singing, too, softly, trying to sound like Crosby, with the bub-bub-bub-boos thrown in. I put a hand under the table and on Hilda's thigh. She didn't move or say anything and I kept my hand there, feeling the long, smooth curved flesh under the dress.

'You girls doing anything tonight?' I asked.

'I don't think so,' Hilda reckoned, looking at Dolores for confirmation.

'No,' the girl called Dolores said. She had a dark, smooth skin and her lipstick was smeared a little. There were small plastic flowers attached to the lobes of her ears and her hair was black and shiny with oil.

'Let's go to the Emperor,' Banjo said.

'What's playing?' Dolores asked?

'A Alan Ladd piece,' Banjo said. 'Real awake. You want to go?'

'Okay. But we don't want you spend your money on us.'

Banjo laughed and said, 'Don't worry about us. We in the chips. Don't I say, pally?'

'You telling me,' I said.

'Where you working?' Hilda asked.

'He works in a facktry,' I told her. 'I'm a messenger.'

'My father is also a messenger,' Hilda said. 'He worked forty years for the firm. Now he's head messenger. Last year they gave him a silver tray with his name out on it, and 'For service-something.'

'For services rendered,' I said.

'You clever,' Hilda said, smiling at me.

'He went to high school,' Banjo told her.

'My ma put the tray on the sideboard,' Hilda said.

'Well,' Dolores announced, 'We got to go home and get ourselves right for the bio.'

'Where are we going to get you?' Banjo asked.

'Get us outside the Emperor. Half past-seven.'

'I think that's okay.'

'We better go now,' Hilda said.

I gave her thigh a squeeze to take the place of a kiss and we all got up. Dolores said thanks for the cold drinks and we went to the door of the cafe with them. Hilda was tall and not too bad, and the pimples didn't matter much. The fat Portagee was behind the counter doing something, and he did not look up as we went out.

The Gladiators

You know mos how it feel when you waiting for your boy to go in and you don't know how he's going to come out. Well, we was feeling the same way that night. We had the bandages on and wait around for the preliminaries to make finish, smoking nervous like and looking at Kenny. He just sit on the table with his legs hanging down, waiting like us, but not nervous like, only full up to his ears with his brag. He's a good juba awright. Build like a bear if you ever see one, with sloping shoulders and big chest, and arms and thighs like polish teak. Not exactly like teak, because he's lighter, just miss being white which was what make him so full of crap. He was sorry he wasn't white and glad he wasn't black. He got a nice face, too, except for the nose that's a little flat from being hit on it a lot, almost like a black boy's nose, but not exactly. Anyway, he's full of crap, that white crap, and me and Gogs is worried because here he is waiting to go in and fight that black boy and we know he's going to try to be mean and do something foolish that might lose him the fight.

We in the dressing room they rig up right next to the lavatory and there's a smell of piss and tobacco and some of that dagga the hard boys must been smoking next door. Outside the hall was book out and we could hear the crowd groaning at the prelims so I reckon they wasn't getting their money's worth.

'How you feeling, Ken?' Gogs beckons to him. He called Gogs because he mos wear those big spectacles.

'I feel first class,' Kenny reckon. He grin and show his teeth and is just like this: 'I'll muck that black bastard.'

I reckon, 'Look, Kenny, you don't have that. Christ, we all blerry black, even if we off-white or like coffee. Be a blerry sport, man.'

'Muck,' Kenny reckon. 'Sport. Awright. It's sport. But what the hell I got to fight black boys and coloured all the time?'

'You want to fight a white boy you got to go to England,' Gogs is just so to him.

'Or Lourenço Marques,' I reckon. 'You know you can't fight no white john here. So just do your best like a sporting ou, hey?'

Kenny laughed at us and reckons, 'You rookers. I'll fight in England yet. You see.'

'Now you don't try nothing fancy in there, hey?' Gogs reckon to him. 'Just go in there and do it like it got to be done.'

'Awright, man, forget it.'

'Okay. Now you shape up okay, so don't muck it just because you fed up with fighting your own kind.'

'Listen,' Kenny reckon to us again. 'Muck that own kind. That boy ain't our kind.'

'Awright,' I say. 'But we all get kicked in the arse the same.'

'For Chrise sake,' Gogs reckon, looking cross. 'We had this blerry crap before. Now let's think about the blerry fight.'

'I'll make the Empire yet,' Kenny reckon. 'You jubas see.'

The crowd is just buzzing and talking now so we reckon the prelims is over. We didn't hear the final gong because why we was talking all this stuff, see? But the door open Noor Abbas who is promoting the show come in. He got on a black dress suit and look just like a head waiter, and he is smoking a cigar.

'Okay,' he reckon to us. 'You on next so shake it up.'

He go out again and Farny push past him into the room. 'Awright, let's go.'

Kenny get off the table and we hang the dressing gown over his shoulders. It was orange colour with Kid Kenny in brown letters on the back. I reckon it was a real smart gown.

'You okay?' Farny ask him as we go out.

'I'll moider him,' Kenny reckon.

'Who you think you is—Kirk Douglas?' Gogs reckon, laughing like.

'He think he's Louis,' I say. 'Only Louis is black. He don't like black boys. Maybe he reckon he's Potty.'

'Muck him,' Kenny say. 'That boer.'

'Awright . . . Marciano,' I say.

'Shut up, you rookers,' Farny reckon.

We go down the aisle between the high, sloping tiers of seats built up on tubular scaffolding and the black boy is just climbing into the ring. He didn't get a big hand. He was a good-looking boy with a dark, shiny skin and thick chest. He bounce around the ring a little and the crowd laugh. I thought, what a country. The black boy had a white robe on him with a real smart tiger work out in black across the back. He was the Black Panther on the posters, but I forget his right name now.

Further, when we come up the aisle the crowd start yelling and clapping when they see Kenny and he grin, braggy like, and we go through the ringside chairs to the ring. The crowd was mostly men with some goosies in among them and they shout themselves hoarse for Kenny and he climb up through the ropes and wave to them.

I'm just like this to Gogs, 'This sonovabitch act like blerry Gentleman Jim Corbett himself. I bet he reckon he's fighting the world heavyweight.'

'Hell, he's okay,' Gogs reckon. 'He just a little full of up-say. That's all.'

Kenny hold his hands together and shake them over his head to the crowd like the champion in the beece, which is what we call a cinema, and everybody give him a clap. Then he sit down and the Panther's boy come over and say Hello, and look at the tape and then we pull the gloves on, working them onto his hands and tying the strings good.

Gogs reckon, 'Now you don't do nothing smart, Kenny.'

'Ach, you jubas,' he reckon and wave his gloves at us.

I look across at the Panther and he a tall john with one-forty stretch over six-feet of framework and cover with a blue-black skin.

The ref call them to the centre and tell them the rules and Kenny come back saying, 'That tsotsi, that tsotsi.'

'Take it easy with him,' I reckon. 'He look like he got a blerry long reach.'

'Watch me bugger him. That tsotsi,' Kenny reckon.

I take the dressing gown off him and he smile around. Somebody yell, Donder that k———r. I look across to see who it is but there only five thousands pack into the hall, all waiting for them to hit each other to mince. There some white boys out front in the ring-sides, smiling and talking, and all over there's a haze of blue-grey tobacco smoke.

The hall lights go mos down and the lights over the ring stay on, so you only see the fighters and the ref, and the whole crowd is quiet like, waiting to see blood. I thought, Bastards, paying cash to see two other black boys knock themselves to hell. What you in this business for then? I don't know. Maybe just to see my boy don't get buggered too much.

The gong go and we get out quick, Gogs carrying the stool, and we down there watching our boy go in.

In the big ring lights the fighter, Kenny pale, almost white, and the black boy, tall, move up towards each other careful like, and touch gloves, and as soon as the Panther drop his hands Kenny hit him twice in the face with the left and jump back. Kenny box good, but the Panther is a dancer, crouching and bobbing.

Three four times Kenny bring his left over but the Panther take it on the shoulders or the arms. He don't seem to care about that left. He just bob and duck and keep those lefts off his face, and after a while the crowd is yelling at him to go in and fight.

Further, Kenny just stay in there knocking up points and for the next three rounds it is all his. Back in the corner he smile at us as we work on him, saying, 'You see me floor that blerry tsotsi.'

In the fourth he go in like he's going to finish the fight right then, and the Panther just let him come, dancing around and holding his gloves up so you can see the white of his eyes and his black shiny face between them. The crowd is stamping and shouting for Kenny to go in and make him finish so they can go home. They was sure hoping to see the black boy go down.

Well, the Panther just let Kenny come and even drop his guard. Kenny's left come in, but the Panther just shift his head and let the glove go past and then he hit Kenny you can hear it outside.

That surprise Kenny and you can see it on his face and the Panther hit him again, and man, this time you can hear it down by the railway station, and then the blerry Panther dance away, like this, bobbing and dancing and waiting for Kenny to come after him and Kenny the blerry fool, go after him and the Panther hit him one two three and there's big red patches on all two sides of him, under his ribs, and he look plenty shaken. Kenny come after the Panther again and the Panther go in and meet him this time, dancing forward, and Kenny reach out with the left and the Panther take it on the right shoulder and jab Kenny twice with his right in the ribs and now the crowd is yelling for the black boy to give it to him.

After the fifth Farny is worried and is just like this to Kenny, 'Listen, man, take your time. That juba is a fighter, and you got to wear him down. You not going to floor him right off like that. Take your time man.'

'That black piece of crap,' Kenny reckon, sounding like a damaged boiler. 'The hell with him.'

Farny shake his head and look at us. I think, I'm leaving this blerry play-white penny-ha'penny braggard alone after this. Muck him.

Further, in the sixth round they get tied up and Kenny try to get loose of the clinch but the Panther come up with a uppercut that take him on the nose. Kenny's nose bleed and he try to lean on the Panther but the Panther shake him off and hit him again in the same spot and Kenny got back shaking his head like he can't see a damn thing and the Panther come after him, dancing, and hit him again and again. There blood all over Kenny's face and he wipe it away with a glove. The black boy come after him again, but the gong go and we take Kenny back to our corner.

He got a nose like a doughnut, but he wave us off after we wash it. He was a hardcase john awright. I give him that.

'That bastard can't do this to me,' he reckon.

'How you feeling?' Gogs ask.

'Any more like that and I throw the towel in,' Farny reckon.

'The hell with you,' Kenny reckon to him, 'I'll make that boy kneel.'

The gong go again and the crowd is screaming you can't hear a thing. Kenny go in there but you can see he's more careful now, watching like, and the Panther watch him, too, waiting, dancing and bobbing, his long body shiny with sweat. The crowd get quiet and everybody is waiting to see what going to happen. The two of them, Kenny and the black boy, just circle around, waiting for a opening.

Well, Kenny got some trouble with his nose and keep on dabbing it with a glove. He wait for an opening and the Panther feint with his right and Kenny falls for it, knocking the glove aside and the next thing the Panther hit him right in the V of the solar plexus. It was some blow. I reckon the eyes was coming out of Kenny's head. He look pop-eyed and while he's holding onto his body the Panther hit him on the nose again and then in the mouth and another one in the mouth and the blood run and Kenny is just staggering around with the Panther coming after hitting him one two one two one two one two like he was working on the heavy bag.

Now there's no more shouting, just one solid noise of the mob. They all on their feet, screaming because they seen blood and they all gone mad with seeing it, because they seeing a man hit to a bloody mess. They don't give a damn about Kenny no more now, and they don't give a damn about nothing but seeing his blood.

Further, Farny is ready with the towel now, but he can't make up his mind to throw it in, looking at Kenny and waiting for the gong to save him or something. But the Panther come after Kenny all the time and hit him one two one two, and the next thing Kenny's down on his knees, one hand waving slowly about like it was looking for something to hang onto, then he's down up there and the ref is taking the count.

Well, the black boy wins it on a knock-out and the time we get Kenny round the crowd is moving out and looking at us as they pass the ring, climbing over the chairs. Kenny come to, his face a mess and his mouth swell up like a couple of polonies, and we get him up between us. Farny is talking to the Panther's people, and we help Kenny down to the floor and go on out towards the dressing-room with him between us, through the last remains of the crowd and the crunch peanut shells and crush cigarette ends.

Blankets

Choker lay on the floor of the lean-to in the back yard where they had carried him. It was cooler under the sagging roof, with the pile of assorted junk in one corner; an ancient motor tyre, sundry split and warped boxes, an old enamel display sign with patches like maps of continents on another planet where the enamelling had cracked away, and the dusty footboard of a bed. There was also the smell of dust and chicken droppings and urine in the lean-to.

From outside, beyond a chrome-yellow rhomboid of sun, came a clatter of voices. In the yard they were discussing him. Choker opened his eyes, and peering down the length of his body, past the bare, grimy toes, he saw several pairs of legs, male and female, in tattered trousers and laddered stockings.

Somebody, a man, was saying: '. . . that was coward . . . from behind, mos.'

'Ja. But look what he done to others . . .'

Choker thought, to hell with those baskets. To hell with them all.

Somebody had thrown an old blanket over him. It smelled of

sweat and having-been-slept-in-unwashed, and it was torn and threadbare and stained. He touched the exhausted blanket with thick, grubby fingers. The texture was rough in parts and shiny thin where it had worn away. He was used to blankets like this.

Choker had been stabbed three times, each time from behind. Once in the head, then between the shoulder blades and again in the right side, out in the street, by an old enemy who had once sworn to get him.

The bleeding had stopped and there was not much pain. He had been knifed before, admittedly not as bad as this, but he thought through the pain, The basket couldn't even do a decent job. He lay there and waited for the ambulance. There was blood drying slowly on the side of his hammered-copper face, and he also had a bad headache.

The voices, now and then raised in laughter, crackled outside. Feet moved on the rough floor of the yard and a face not unlike that of a brown dog wearing an expiring cloth cap, looked in.

'You still awright, Choker? Am'ulance is coming just now, hey.'

'——— off', Choker said. His voice croaked.

The face withdrew, laughing: 'Ou Choker. Ou Choker.'

He was feeling tired now. The grubby fingers, like corroded iron clamps, strayed over the parched field of the blanket . . . He was being taken down a wet, tarred yard with tough wire netting over the windows which looked into it. The place smelled of carbolic disinfectant, and the bunch of heavy keys clink-clinked as it swung from the hooked finger of the guard.

They reached a room fitted with shelving that was stacked here and there with piled blankets. 'Take two, jong,' the guard said, and Choker began to rummage through the piles, searching for the thickest and warmest blankets. But the guard, who somehow had a doggish face and wore a disintegrating cloth cap, laughed and jerked him aside, and seizing the nearest blankets, found two and flung them at Choker. They were filthy and smelly and within their folds vermin waited like irregular troops in ambush.

'Come on. Come on. You think I got time to waste?'

'It's cold, mos, man,' Choker said. But it wasn't the guard to whom he was talking. He was six years old and his brother, Willie, a year senior, twisted and turned in the narrow, cramped, sagging bedstead which they shared, dragging the thin cotton blanket from Choker's body. Outside the rain slapped against the cardboard-patched window, and the wind wheezed through cracks and corners like an asthmatic old man.

'No, man, Willie, man. You got all the blanket, jong.'

'Well, I can't mos help it, man. It's cold.'

'What about me?' Choker whined. 'What about me. I'm also cold mos.'

Huddled together under the blanket, fitted against each other like two pieces of a jigsaw puzzle. The woman's wiry hair got into his mouth and smelled of stale brilliantine. There were dark stains made by heads, on the crumpled, grey-white pillow, and a rubbed smear of lipstick, like a half-healed wound.

The woman was saying, half-asleep, 'No, man. No, man.' Her body was wet and sweaty under the blanket, and the bed smelled of a mixture of cheap perfume, spilled powder, human bodies and infant urine. The faded curtain over a window beckoned to him in the hot breeze. In the early slum-coloured light a torn under-garment hanging from a brass knob was a spectre in the room.

The woman turned from him under the blankets, protesting, and Choker sat up. The agonized sounds of the bedspring woke the baby in the bathtub on the floor, and it began to cry, its toothless voice rising in a high-pitched wail that grew louder and louder . . .

Choker opened his eyes as the wail grew to a crescendo and then quickly faded as the siren was switched off. Voices still splattered the sunlight in the yard, now excited. Choker saw the skirts of white coats and then the ambulance men were in the lean-to. His head was aching badly, and his wounds were throbbing. His face perspired like a squeezed-out wash-rag. Hands searched him. One of the ambulance attendants asked: 'Do you feel any pain?

Choker looked at the pink-white face above his, scowling. 'No, sir.'

The layer of old newspapers on which he was lying was soaked with his blood. 'Knife wounds,' one of the attendants said. 'He isn't bleeding much,' the other said. 'Put on a couple of pressure pads.'

He was in mid-air, carried on a stretcher and flanked by a procession of onlookers. Rubber sheeting was cool against his back. The stretcher rumbled into the ambulance and the doors slammed shut, sealing off the spectators. Then the siren whined and rose, clearing a path through the crowd.

Choker felt the vibration of the ambulance through his body as it sped on its way. His murderous fingers touched the folded edge of the bedding. The sheet around him was white as cocaine, and the blanket was thick and new and warm. He lay still, listening to the siren.

A Matter of Taste

The sun hung well towards the west now so that the thin clouds above the ragged horizon were rimmed with bright yellow like the spilt yolk of an egg. Chinaboy stood up from having blown the fire under the round tin and said, 'She ought to boil now.' The tin stood precariously balanced on two half-bricks and a smooth stone. We had built the fire carefully in order to brew some coffee and now watched the water in the tin with the interest of women at a child-birth.

'There she is,' Chinaboy said as the surface broke into bubbles. He waited for the water to boil up and then drew a small crushed packet from the side pocket of his shredded wind-breaker, un-twisted its mouth and carefully tapped raw coffee into the tin.

He was a short man with grey-flecked kinky hair, and a wide, quiet, heavy face that had a look of patience about it, as if he had grown accustomed to doing things slowly and carefully and correctly. But his eyes were dark oriental ovals, restless as a pair of cockroaches.

'We'll let her draw a while,' he advised. He put the packet away and produced an old rag from another pocket, wrapped it around a hand and gingerly lifted the tin from the fire, placing it carefully in the sand near the bricks.

We had just finished a job for the railways and were camped out a few yards from the embankment and some distance from the ruins of a onetime siding. The corrugated iron of the office still stood, gaping in places and covered with rust and cobwebs. Passers had fouled the roofless interior and the platform was crumbled in places and overgrown with weeds. The cement curbing still stood, but cracked and covered with the disintegration like a welcome notice to a ghost town. Chinaboy got out the scoured condensed-milk tins we used for cups and set them up. I sat on an old sleeper and waited for the ceremony of pouring the coffee to commence.

It didn't start right then because Chinaboy was crouching with his rag-wrapped hand poised over the can, about to pick it up, but he wasn't making a move. Just sitting like that and watching something beyond us.

The portjackson bush and wattle crackled and rustled behind me and the long shadow of a man fell across the small clearing. I looked back and up. He had come out of the plantation and was thin and short and had a pale white face covered with a fine golden stubble. Dirt lay in dark lines in the creases around his mouth and under his eyes and in his neck, and his hair was ragged and thick and uncut, falling back to his neck and around his temples. He wore an old pair of jeans, faded and dirty and turned up at the bottoms, and a torn leather coat.

He stood on the edge of the clearing, waiting hesitantly, glancing from me to Chinaboy, and then back at me. He ran the back of a grimy hand across his mouth.

Then he said hesitantly: 'I smelled the coffee. Hope you don' min'.' 'Well,' Chinaboy said with that quiet careful smile of his.

'Seeing you's here, I reckon I don' min' either.' He smiled at me, 'you think we can take in a table boarder, pal?'

'Reckon we can spare some of the turkey and green peas.'

Chinaboy nodded at the stranger. 'Sit, pally. We were just going to have supper.'

The white boy grinned a little embarrassedly and came around the sleeper and shoved a rock over with a scarred boot and straddled it. He didn't say anything, but watched as Chinaboy set out another scoured milk-tin and lift the can from the fire and pour the coffee into the cups.

'Help yourself, man. Isn't exactly the mayor's garden party.' The boy took his cup carefully and blew at the steam. Chinaboy sipped noisily and said, 'Should've had some bake bread. Nothing like a piece of bake bread with cawfee.'

'Hot dogs,' the white boy said.

'Huh.'

'Hot dogs. Hot dogs go with coffee.'

'Ooh ja. I heard,' Chinaboy grinned. Then he asked: 'You going somewhere, Whitey?'

'Cape Town. Maybe get a job on a ship an' make the States.'

'Lots of people want to reach the States,' I said.

Whitey drank some coffee and said: 'Yes, I heard there's plenty of money and plenty to eat.'

'Talking about eating,' Chinaboy said: 'I see a picture in a book, one time. 'Merican Book. This picture was about food over there. A whole mess of fried chicken, mealies—what they call corn—with mushrooms an' gravy, chips and new green peas. All done up in colours, too.

'Pass me the roast lamb,' I said sarcastically.

'Man,' Whitey said warming up to the discussion 'Just let me get to something like that and I'll eat till I burst wide open.'

Chinaboy swallowed some coffee: 'Worked as a waiter one time when I was a youngster. In one of that big caffies. You should've seen what all them bastards ate. Just sitting there shovelling it down. Some French stuff too, patty grass or something like that.'

I said: 'Remember the time we went for drunk and got ten days? We ate mealies and beans till it came out of our ears!'

Chinaboy said, whimsically: 'I'd like to sit down in a smart caffy one day and eat my way right out of a load of turkey, roast potatoes, beet-salad and angel's food trifle. With port and cigars at the end.'

'Hell,' said Whitey, 'it's all a matter of taste. Some people like chicken and othe's eat sheep's heads and beans!'

'A matter of taste,' Chinaboy scowled. 'Bull, it's a matter of money, pal. I worked six months in that caffy and I never heard nobody order sheep's head and beans!'

'You heard of the fellow who went into one of these big caffies?' Whitey asked, whirling the last of this coffee around in the tin cup. 'He sits down at a table and takes out a packet of sandwiches and puts it down. Then he calls the waiter and orders a glass of water. When the waiter brings the water, this fellow says: "Why ain't the band playing?" '

We chuckled over that and Chinaboy almost choked. He coughed and spluttered a little and then said, 'Another John goes into a caffy and orders sausage and mash. When the waiter bring him the stuff he take a look and say: "My dear man, you've brought me a cracked plate." "Hell," says the waiter. "That's no crack. That's the sausage".'

After we had laughed over that one Chinaboy looked westward at the sky. The sun was almost down and the clouds hung like bloodstained rags along the horizon. There was a breeze stirring the wattle and portjackson, and far beyond the railway line.

A dog barked with high yapping sounds.

Chinaboy said: 'There's a empty goods going through here

around about seven. We'll help Whitey, here, onto it, so's he can get to Cape Town. Reckon there's still time for some more pork chops and onions.' He grinned at Whitey. 'Soon's we've had dessert we'll walk down the line a little. There's a bend where it's the best place to jump a train. We'll show you.'

He waved elaborately towards me: 'Serve the duck, John!'

I poured the last of the coffee into the tin cups. The fire had died to a small heap of embers. Whitey dug in the pocket of his leather coat and found a crumpled pack of cigarettes. There were just three left and he passed them round. We each took one and Chinaboy lifted the twig from the fire and we lighted up.

'Good cigar, this,' he said, examining the glowing tip of the cigarette.

When the coffee and cigarettes were finished, the sun had gone down altogether, and all over the land was swept with dark shadows of a purple hue. The silhouetted tops of the wattle and portjackson looked like massed dragons.

We walked along the embankment in the evening, past the ruined siding, the shell of the station-house like a huge desecrated tombstone against the sky. Far off we heard the whistle of a train.

'This is the place,' Chinaboy said to Whitey. 'It's a long goods and when she takes the turn the engine driver won't see you, and neither the rooker in the guard's van. You got to jump when the engine's out of sight. She'll take the hill slow likely, so you'll have a good chance. Jus' you wait till I say when. Hell, that sound like pouring a drink!' His teeth flashed in the gloom as he grinned. Then Whitey stuck out a hand and Chinaboy shook it, and then I shook it.

'Thanks for supper, boys,' Whitey said.

'Come again, anytime,' I said, 'we'll see we have a tablecloth.' We waited in the portjackson growth at the side of the embankment while the goods train wheezed and puffed up the grade, its headlamp cutting a big yellow hole in the dark. We ducked back out of sight as the locomotive went by, hissing and rumbling. The tender followed, then a couple of box-cars, then some coal-cars and a flat-car, another box-car. The locomotive was out of sight.

'Here it is,' Chinaboy said pushing the boy ahead. We stood near the train, hearing it click-clack past. 'Take this coal box coming up,' Chinaboy instructed. 'She's low and empty. Don't miss the grip, now. She's slow. And good luck, pal!'

The coal-car came up and Whitey moved out, watching the iron grip on the far end of it. Then as it drew slowly level with him, he reached out, grabbed and hung on, then got a foothold, moving away from us slowly.

We watched him hanging there, reaching for the edge of the car and hauling himself up. Watching the train clicking away, we saw him straddling the edge of the truck, his hand raised in a salute. We raised our hands too.

'Why ain't the band playing? Hell!' Chinaboy said.

The Lemon Orchard

The men came down between two long, regular rows of trees. The winter had not passed completely and there was a chill in the air; and the moon was hidden behind long, high parallels of cloud which hung like suspended streamers of dirty cotton-wool in the sky. All of the men but one wore thick clothes against the coolness of the night. The night and earth was cold and damp, and the shoes of the men sank into the soil and left exact, ridged foot prints, but they could not be seen in the dark.

One of the men walked ahead holding a small cycle lantern that worked from a battery, leading the way down the avenue of trees while the others came behind in the dark. The night close around was quiet now that the crickets had stopped their small noises, but far out others that did not feel the presence of the men continued the monotonous creek-creek-creek. Somewhere, even further, a dog started barking in short high yaps, and then stopped abruptly. The men were walking through an orchard of lemons and the sharp, bitter-sweet citrus smell hung gently on the night air.

'Do not go so fast,' the man who brought up the rear of the party called to the man with the lantern. 'It's as dark as a kaffir's soul here at the back.'

He called softly, as if the darkness demanded silence. He was a big man and wore khaki trousers and laced-up riding boots, and an old shooting jacket with leather patches on the right breast and the elbows.

The shotgun was loaded. In the dark this man's face was invisible except for a blur of shadowed hollows and lighter crags. Although he walked in the rear he was the leader of the party. The lantern-bearer slowed down for the rest to catch up with him.

'It's cold, too, Oom,' another man said.

'Cold?' the man with the shotgun asked, speaking with sarcasm. 'Are you colder than this verdomte hotnot, here?' And he gestured in the dark with the muzzle of the gun at the man who stumbled along in their midst and who was the only one not warmly dressed.

This man wore trousers and a raincoat which they had allowed him to pull on over his pyjamas when they had taken him from his lodgings, and he shivered now with chill, clenching his teeth to prevent them from chattering. He had not been given time to tie his shoes and the metal-covered ends of the laces clicked as he moved.

'Are you cold, hotnot?' the man with the light jeered.

The coloured man did not reply. He was afraid, but his fear was mixed with a stubbornness which forbade him to answer them.

'He is not cold,' the fifth man in the party said. 'He is shivering with fear. Is it not so, hotnot?'

The coloured man said nothing, but stared ahead of himself into the half-light made by the small lantern. He could see the silhouette of the man who carried the light, but he did not want to look at the two who flanked him, the one who had complained of the cold, and the one who had spoken of his fear. They each carried a sjambok and every now and then one of them slapped a corduroyed leg with his.

'He is dumb also,' the one who had spoken last chuckled.

'No, Andries. Wait a minute,' the leader who carried the shotgun said, and they all stopped between the row of trees. The man with the lantern turned and put the light on the rest of the party.

'What is it?' he asked.

'Wag'n oomblikkie. Wait a moment,' the leader said, speaking with forced casualness. 'He is not dumb. He is a slim hotnot; one of those educated bushmen. Listen, hotnot,' he addressed the coloured man, speaking angrily now. 'When a baas speaks to you, you answer him. Do you hear?' The coloured man's wrists were tied behind him with a riem and the leader brought the muzzle of the shotgun down, pressing it hard into the small of the man's back above where the wrists met. 'Do you hear, hotnot? Answer me or I will shoot a hole through your spine.'

The bound man felt the hard round metal of the gun muzzle through the loose raincoat and clenched his teeth. He was cold and tried to prevent himself from shivering in case it should be mistaken for cowardice. He heard the small metallic noise as the man with the gun thumbed back the hammer of the shotgun. In spite of the cold little drops of sweat began to form on his upper lip under the overnight stubble.

'For God's sake, don't shoot him,' the man with the light said, laughing a little nervously. 'We don't want to be involved in any murder.'

'What are you saying, man?' the leader asked. Now with the beam of the battery-lamp on his face the shadows in it were washed away to reveal the mass of tiny wrinkled and deep creases which covered the red-clay complexion of his face like the myriad lines which indicate rivers, streams, roads and railways on a map. They wound around the ridges of his chin and climbed the sharp range of his nose and the peaks of his chin and cheekbones, and his eyes were hard and blue like two frozen lakes.

'This is mos a slim hotnot,' he said again. 'A teacher in a school for which we pay. He lives off our sweat, and he had the audacity to be cheeky and uncivilized towards a minister of our church and no hotnot will be cheeky to a white man while I live.'

'Ja, man,' the lantern-bearer agreed. 'But we are going to deal with him. There is no necessity to shoot him. We don't want that kind of trouble.'

'I will shoot whatever hotnot or kaffir I desire, and see me get into trouble over it. I demand respect from these donders. Let them answer when they're spoken to.'

He jabbed the muzzle suddenly into the coloured man's back so that he stumbled struggling to keep his balance. 'Do you hear, jong? Did I not speak to you?' The man who had jeered about the prisoner's fear stepped up then, and hit him in the face, striking him on a cheekbone with the clenched fist which still held the sjambok. He was angry over the delay and wanted the man to submit so that they could proceed. 'Listen you hotnot bastard,' he said loudly. 'Why don't you answer?'

The man stumbled, caught himself and stood in the rambling shadow of one of the lemon trees. The lantern-light swung on him and he looked away from the centre of the beam. He was afraid the leader would shoot him in anger and he had no wish to die. He straightened up and looked away from them.

'Well?' demanded the man who had struck him.

'Yes, baas,' the bound man said, speaking with a mixture of dignity and contempt which was missed by those who surrounded him.

'Yes there,' the man with the light said. 'You could save yourself trouble. Next time you will remember. Now let us get on.' The lantern swung forward again and he walked ahead. The leader shoved their prisoner on with the muzzle of the shotgun, and he stumbled after the bobbing lantern with the other men on each side of him.

'The amazing thing about it is that this bliksem should have taken the principal, and the meester of the church before the magistrate and demand payment for the hiding they gave him for being cheeky to them,' the leader said to all in general. 'This verdomte hotnot. I have never heard of such a thing in all my born days.'

'Well, we will give him a better hiding,' the man, Andries said. 'This time we will teach him a lesson, Oom. He won't demand damages from anybody when we're done with him.'

'And afterwards he won't be seen around here again. He will pack his things and go and live in the city where they're not so particular about the dignity of the volk. Do you hear, hotnot?' This time they were not concerned about receiving a reply but the leader went on, saying, 'We don't want any educated hottentots in our town.'

'Neither black Englishmen,' added one of the others.

The dog started barking again at the farm house which was invisible on the dark hillside at the other end of the little valley. 'It's that Jagter,' the man with the lantern said. 'I wonder what bothers him. He is a good watch-dog. I offered Meneer Marais five pounds for that dog, but he won't sell. I would like to have a dog like that. I would take great care of such a dog.'

The blackness of the night crouched over the orchard and the leaves rustled with a harsh whispering that was inconsistent with the pleasant scent of the lemons. The chill in the air had increased, and far-off the creek-creek-creek of the crickets blended into solid strips of high-pitched sound. Then the moon came from behind the banks of cloud and its white light touched the leaves with wet silver, and the perfume of lemons seemed to grow stronger, as if the juice was being crushed from them.

They walked a little way further in the moonlight and the man with the lantern said, 'This is as good a place as any, Oom.'

They had come into a wide gap in the orchard, a small amphitheatre surrounded by fragrant growth, and they all stopped within it. The moonlight clung for a while to the leaves and the angled branches, so that along their tips and edges the moisture gleamed with the quivering shine of scattered quicksilver.